STUDY GUIDE

Music

FOURTH EDITION

STUDY GUIDE

RAYMOND BARR
University of Miami

Music

FOURTH EDITION

DANIEL T. POLITOSKE
University of Kansas

ART ESSAYS BY MARTIN WERNER
Temple University

PRENTICE HALL
Englewood Cliffs, New Jersey 07632

Editorial/production supervision and
   interior design: Jacqueline Vernaglia
Manufacturing buyer: Ray Keating

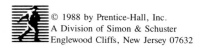 © 1988 by Prentice-Hall, Inc.
A Division of Simon & Schuster
Englewood Cliffs, New Jersey 07632

Printed in the United States of America

10   9   8   7   6   5   4   3   2   1

0-13-607698-X

Prentice-Hall International (UK) Limited, *London*
Prentice-Hall of Australia Pty. Limited, *Sydney*
Prentice-Hall Canada Inc., *Toronto*
Prentice-Hall Hispanoamericana, S.A., *Mexico*
Prentice-Hall of India Private Limited, *New Delhi*
Prentice-Hall of Japan, Inc., *Tokyo*
Simon & Schuster Asia Pte. Ltd., *Singapore*
Editora Prentice-Hall do Brasil, Ltda., *Rio de Janeiro*

Contents

Preface

The best way to use this Study Guide is to first carefully read the chapter of the textbook relating to the corresponding chapter in the Study Guide. Read the chapter carefully, underlining or highlighting terms, concepts, titles and names you consider to be important as you read. Also, you might make an outline of the chapter as you read it, or put down important facts on note cards for later study and reference.

Having done this, and ONLY after having done this, turn to the chapter in the Study Guide relating to the chapter in the Textbook you have studied and answer the questions to the best of your ability WITHOUT using any of your notes. Then, use your notes, outline or note cards to find any answers you could not remember. As a final check, compare your answers to the textbook chapter itself to make sure you have the correct answers to all of the questions.

The worst way to use this Study Guide is simply to copy the answers into the Study Guide directly from the textbook chapters, because if you do so, you will not be able to discover what you know and what you do not know, and you will not be preparing yourself for actual tests and examinations, which is one of the main purposes of having a study guide.

The listening questions found in each chapter of the Study Guide will help you to know what to listen for when you are listening to the various items on the record set which relate to each chapter of the textbook. Listening with these guidelines should greatly improve your listening habits and develop in you the ability to get the most out of any music you listen to.

Finally, there are self-tests for each section of the textbook as well as for each chapter. These tests should be approached in the same way as described above for the chapter tests. If the chapter tests are worked on properly, the sectional tests should be relatively easy to answer, since the information in them is taken from the chapter tests themselves.

Good reading! Good listening! Good studying! ENJOY!!

STUDY GUIDE

Music

FOURTH EDITION

CHAPTER 1

Melody and Rhythm

<u>KEY TERMS AND CONCEPTS</u>

THE BASIC MATERIALS OF MUSIC: SOUND AND TIME

A. MUSICAL SOUND
   1. Musical tones
   2. Pitch
      a. Notes
      b. Staff
      c. Ascending Tones
      d. Descending tones
   3. Melody
      a. Disjunct melodies
      b. Conjunct melodies
   4. Melodic Structure
      a. Contrast
      b. Repetition
      c. Phrases
   5. Melodic Patterns
B. RHYTHM
   1. Rhythmic Patterns
   2. Meter
      a. Beats
      b. Accent
      c. Duple meter
      d. Triple meter
      e. Measure
      f. Simple meter
      g. Compound meter
      h. Syncopation
   3. Rhythmic Expression

4. Tempo
   a. Tempo markings
   b. Accelerando
   c. Ritardando

COMPLETE THE FOLLOWING:

1. In a musical tone, the number of vibrations that occur per second determines a property called _____.

2. The written form of musical tones are called _____.

3. Written music consists of oval symbols arranged on a sort of linear ladder called a _____.

4. A succession of musical tones used in a meaningful way is called a _____.

5. A musical line in which there are large distances between successive tones is called a _____.

6. A musical line that moves in small steps is called a _____ _____.

7. Two basic elements of good melodic structure are _____ _____ and _____.

8. The standard melodic unit is called a _____.

9. The organizing principle of music within time is known as _____.

10. The pattern of accented and unaccented beats or pulses in music is called _____.

11. If the beats or pulses of a piece of music fall into patterns of two, or a multiple of two, the music is said to be in _____ meter.

12. If the beats of pulses of a piece of music fall into patterns of three, or a multiple of three, the music is said to be in _____ meter.

13. Music is structured in groups of beats or pulses known as _____.

14. The speed at which music is performed is referred to as _____.

15. Gradual speeding up within a musical composition is referred to as _____, whereas gradual

2

slowing down is known as _____ or
_____ .

FOR EACH OF THE FOLLOWING TEMPO MARKINGS, INDICATE WHETHER
EACH INDICATES THAT THE MUSIC IS TO BE PERFORMED VERY
SLOWLY (VS), SLOWLY (S), MODERATELY (M), FAST (F) OR VERY
FAST (VF)

1. _____ Lento   6. _____ Adagio
2. _____ Presto   7. _____ Vivace
3. _____ Andante   8. _____ Moderato
4. _____ Grave   9. _____ Largo
5. _____ Allegro   10. _____ Prestissimo

CHAPTER 2

Harmony and Texture

COMPLETE THE FOLLOWING:

1. The sounding together of two or more tones with the consequent effect of adding musical depth and richness, is known as _____ .

2. The combination of two musical tones sounded simultaneously is known as a(n) _____ .

3. The combination of three or more musical tones sounded simultaneously is known as a(n) _____ .

4. In musical composition, the harmony which suggests and enhances the melody is known as the _____ .

5. Intervals and chords which sound pleasing to the ear are said to be _____ , whereas intervals and chords which do not sound pleasing to the ear are said to be _____ .

6. How many musical tones comprise a chromatic scale? _____ .

7. The best-known scale in Western music is the _____ scale.

8. The basic note of a scale, the note on which the scale is built, is known as the _____ .

9. The half steps in a major scale lie between the _____ and _____ note and between the _____ and _____ note.

10. The first, third and fifth note of the major scale, when played together, produce a chord known as a _____ .

11. A chord built on the fourth note of the scale is known as the _____ chord.

12. A chord built on the fifth note of the scale is known as the _____ chord.

13. A melodic or harmonic closing formula in music is known as a _____ .

14. The dominant (V) chord followed by the tonic (I) chord creates a(n) _____ cadence.

15. The subdominant (IV) chord followed by the tonic (I) chord creates a(n) _____ cadence.

16. A note which is foreign to a scale (that is, a note which is not one of the actual notes of the scale) is referred to as a(n) _____.

17. The shifting from one tonality to another within a piece of music is referred to as _____.

18. The interweaving of the horizontal strands of melody and the vertical strands of harmony in a piece of music is known as _____.

19. Music which consists of a single melodic line, without accompaniment, is known as _____.

20. Music which consists of two or more melodic lines is known as _____ or counterpoint.

21. Counterpoint in which the several melodic lines are the same, or very similar, is known as _____ counterpoint.

22. Counterpoint in which the several melodic lines are different from one another is known as _____ counterpoint.

23. The most common texture currently in use consists of a melody accompanied by chord, a texture referred to as _____.

24. Chords which are played as successive single notes, rather than being played simultaneously, are referred to as _____.

25. Much Western music involves a _____ of various musical textures.

WHICH INTERVAL (THIRD, FIFTH, ETC.) IS REPRESENTED
BY EACH OF THE FOLLOWING COMBINATIONS OF NOTES?

1. C to E _____
2. D to A _____
3. C to B _____
4. E to C _____
5. G to A _____
6. A to D _____
7. F to C _____
8. C to D _____
9. F to F _____
10. D to B _____

IN THE TONALITY OF C, SPELL (E-G-B, ETC.) EACH OF
THE FOLLOWING CHORDS:

1. iii _____ _____ _____
2.   vi _____ _____ _____
3.   V _____ _____ _____
4. vii _____ _____ _____
5.   IV _____ _____ _____

CHAPTER 3
Timbre and Dynamics

<u>KEY TERMS AND CONCEPTS</u>

A. TIMBRE
    1. Vocal
        a. Soprano, Mezzo-Soprano, Contralto (Alto)
        b. Tenor, Baritone, Bass
    2. Instrumental
        a. String Instruments (Chordophones)
            (1) Bowed instruments
                (a) Violin, Viola, Violoncello (Cello),
                    Double Bass (Bass)
                (b) Pizzicato
            (2) Plucked instruments
                (a) Guitar, Banjo, Ukelele, Lute
                (b) Harp
        b. Wind Instruments (Aerophones)
            (1) Woodwind Family
                (a) Flute, piccolo
                (b) Double-Reed Instruments
                    (i) Oboe, English Horn, Bassoon,
                      Contrabassoon
                (c) Single-Reed Instruments
                    (i) Clarinet, Saxophone
            (2) Brass Family
                (a) Cup Mouthpieces
                (b) Trumpet, horn (French horn),
                    trombone, tuba
        c. Percussion Instruments
            (1) Idiophones
                (a) Unpitched
                    (i) Gong, cymbal, maracas

                (b) Pitched
                    (i) Xylophone, triangle
          (2) Membranophones
              (a) Unpitched
                    (i) Snare drum, bass drum, tambourine
              (b) Pitched
                    (i) Timpani (Kettle Drums)
      d. Keyboard Instruments
         (1) Harpsichord, Clavichord
         (2) Pipe Organ
         (3) Piano
      e. Older Instruments
         (1) Crumhorn, shawm, recorder
      f. Modern, electronic instruments
         (1) Synthesizers
  B. THE ORCHESTRA
     1. Chamber Ensemble
     2. Orchestration
       a. Score
  C. DYNAMICS
     1. Dynamic Markings
       a. piano, mezzo piano, pianissimo
       b. forte, mezzo forte, fortissimo
       c. aforzando, forte-piano
     2. Crescendo
     3. Decrescendo (Diminuendo)

COMPLETE THE FOLLOWING:

1. The characteristic quality, or tone color, of the sound produced by a voice or instrument is known as _____ _____.

2. The first musical instrument was probably the _____ _____.

3. The range of sounds a person can make with his or her vocal chords, is determined largely by the size of the person's _____.

4. A musical instrument in which the sound is produced by the vibration of strings is often referred to as a(n) _____.

5. A musical instrument in which the sound is produced by the vibration of a column of air within the instrument is often referred to as a(n) _____.

6. Instruments which rely on a drum head as the principal means of creating sound are often referred to as _____ _____.

7. Percussion instruments in which the whole body of the instrument vibrates to produce the sound are often referred to as _____.

8. The art of writing instrumental music to achieve a variety of effects is known as _____.

9. The effect created by different intensities of sound, loudness and softness, is referred to in music as _____ _____.

10. The violins in an orchestra normally are seated at the conductor's _____ side.

PLACE THE FOLLOWING DYNAMIC MARKINGS IN THEIR PROPER ORDER, FROM VERY SOFT TO VERY LOUD:

FORTE, MEZZO PIANO, PIANISSIMO,
MEZZO FORTE, PIANO, FORTISSIMO

1. _____
2. _____
3. _____
4. _____
5. _____
6. _____

INDICATE WHETHER EACH OF THE FOLLOWING INSTRUMENTS IS STRING (S), WOODWIND (W), BRASS (B) OR PERCUSSION (P):

1. _____ Oboe
2. _____ Trombone
3. _____ Viola
4. _____ Timpani
5. _____ Bassoon
6. _____ Cymbals
7. _____ Piccolo
8. _____ Cello
9. _____ Xylophone
10. _____ Trumpet

CHAPTER 4

Introduction to Musical Form and Style

                    concerto (with soloist), overtures
            e. Works for singers (solo)
                (1) Lieder, arias
            f. Works for choirs
                (1) Madrigals, motets, Masses
            g. Works for singers and instruments
                (1) Cantatas, oratorios, operas
    E. MUSICAL STYLE
        1. Medieval (Middle Ages)
        2. Renaissance
        3. Baroque
        4. Classical
        5. Romantic
        6. Twentieth Century

COMPLETE THE FOLLOWING:

1. The overall design of a piece of music is referred to as
    _____, _____, or _____.

2. The two most fundamental principles of musical form are
    _____ and _____.

3. The shortest units of melody are called _____.

4. Longer melodic units, comparable to the lines of most
    poems, are called _____.

5. The form of most songs is built up from _____.

6. Larger segments of songs are called _____.

7. The setting of several stanzas of a poem to the same
    music is known as _____ form.

8. Three-part form in music is known as _____ form.

9. Two-part form in music is known as _____ form.

10. A musical form in which one primary theme recurs, with
    intervening contrasting themes, is known as _____
    form.

11. Stating a musical idea and then repeating it, but varying
    it in such a way that it sounds at once familiar and new
    is the fundamental concept of _____ form.

12. Forms which have no fixed structure are usually referred
    to as _____ forms.

13. Many larger forms, such as symphonies, have several relatively independent sections called _____.

14. Which period of musical style came first, Baroque or Renaissance? _____.

15. Which period of musical style falls entirely within the nineteenth century (1800s)? _____.

PLACE THE FOLLOWING PERIODS OF MUSICAL STYLE IN THEIR PROPER CHRONOLOGICAL ORDER, FROM EARLY TO MOST RECENT:

CLASSICAL, BAROQUE, MEDIAEVAL, ROMANTIC, TWENTIETH CENTURY, RENAISSANCE

_____
_____
_____
_____
_____
_____

USING THE LETTERS "A", "B" AND "C", GRAPH THE FOLLOWING FORMS:

1. Ternary   _____
2. Rondo   _____
3. Binary   _____
4. Variation   _____

CHAPTER 5

Musical Notation

G. TEMPO
   1. Metronome
      a. Metronome markings

COMPLETE THE FOLLOWING:

1. Musical notation indicates two things, _____ and _____.

2. The pitch of a note is shown by its vertical location on a series of horizontal lines called a _____, which is comprised of _____ lines.

3. If a note is too high or too low for the staff, a short line called a _____ line is added above or below the staff to accommodate the note.

4. Appearing at the extreme left of the staff is a musical sign which indicates the pitch of any given note. This sign is called a _____.

5. Two different forms of the musical sign in question four (the preceding question) are the _____ used to indicate higher pitches, and the _____ used to indicate lower pitches.

6. If the above two staffs are placed one below the other, with an extra space between for the ledger line of middle C the result is the _____ staff.

7. Another, less common, clef is the C Clef, variously known as the _____ clef, if it is centered on the third line of the staff, and the _____ clef, if it is centered on the fourth line of the clef. In either case, the line which runs through the center of this clef is identified as _____ _____.

8. The musical symbol # is called a(n) _____ and indicates that the note accompanying that sign should be raised in pitch by a _____ _____.

9. The musical symbol b is called a(n) _____ and indicates that the note accompanying that sign should be lowered in pitch by a _____ _____.

10. The black keys on the piano can be either _____ or _____.

11. The chromatic scale is comprised of _____ notes.

15

12. If a particular note is to be flatted or sharped through-out a piece of music, it is more convenient to place those flats or sharps at the beginning of the clef, rather than repeating them each time those notes appear. This group of flats or sharps is referred to as a(n) _____ _____.

13. Each key signature can represent two related scales, or keys, _____ and _____.

14. Major scales have half-step intervals after the _____ and _____ notes, while minor scales have half-step intervals after the _____ and _____ notes.

15. If a flat or sharp is to be cancelled during the course of a piece of music a musical sign called a(n) _____ is used.

16. Another name for flats and sharps in musical notation is _____.

17. The appearance of a note tells the performer not only its pitch, but also its _____.

18. Groups of notes of smaller value are often linked together with heavy _____ to make them easier to read.

19. Two methods of indicating a duration of a greater length than the value of the note itself are by the use of either a(n) _____ or a(n) _____.

20. Periods of silence in music are indicated by musical symbols called _____.

21. Beats or pulses in music are grouped together in regular groups, of equal length, called _____, which are separated from one another by vertical lines called _____ lines.

22. The lower number of a meter signature shows which note has the value of _____ beat.

23. The upper number of a meter signature shows the number of _____ in a _____.

24. Common time is the equivalent of _____ meter.

25. The tempo, or speed, of a musical composition can be set by using a device called a _____.

GIVE THE EQUIVALENTS FOR EACH OF THE FOLLOWING NOTES:
(EXAMPLE: C# = dB)

1. F# = _____
2. B# = _____
3. Ab = _____
4. Cb = _____
5. E# = _____
6. Db = _____
7. G# = _____
8. A# = _____
9. D# = _____
10. Fb = _____

NAME THE RELATIVE MINOR SCALES OF THE FOLLOWING MAJOR
SCALES:

1. F Major _____
2. C Major _____
3. G Major _____
4. Bb Major _____
5. D Major _____

USING THE TREBLE CLEF, SPELL THE FOLLOWING WORDS,
USING MUSICAL NOTES:

BADGE, BED, CAGE, CAB, BEAD

USING THE BASS CLEF, SPELL THE FOLLOWING WORDS,
USING MUSICAL NOTES:

BEG, AGE, BADE, CEDE, DEAD

17

CHAPTER 6
Medieval Music

C. THE GROWTH OF POLYPHONY
   1. Organus
   2. Tenor and duplus parts
   3. Organum purum style
   4. Discantus style
D. THE MOTET
   1. Combining sacred and secular texts
E. MUSIC OF THE FOURTEENTH CENTURY
   1. Ars Nova
   2. Rhythmic innovations
      a. Use of duple meter
      b. Isorhythm
      c. Rhythmic complexity
F. FOURTEENTH CENTURY SECULAR FORMS
   1. French forms
      a. Rondeau
      b. Virelai
      c. Ballade
      d. Lai
   2. Italian forms
      a. Madrigal
      b. Caccia
      c. Ballata
G. IMPORTANT MEDIEVAL COMPOSERS
   1. Bernart de Ventadorn (c. 1130-1190)
   2. Leonin (fl. 1190)
   3. Perotin (fl. 1200)
   4. Philippe de Vitry (1290-1361)
      a. Ars Nova
   5. Guillaume de Machaut (c. 1300-1377)
      a. Messe de Notre Dame
   6. Francesco Landini (1325-1397)

COMPLETE THE FOLLOWING:

1. The Mediaeval Period begins about the _____ century.

2. The two most important institutions of the Middle Ages were the feudal system and the _____.

3. The majority of music of the Middle Ages was of what type? _____.

4. The most musically elaborate of the Hours of the Divine Office was the evening service known as _____.

5. The heart of the Church rite was the _____, which contained two different kinds of texts, the _____ and the _____.

6. The parts of the Mass which were most often set to music were the _____ _____, the _____, the _____/ _____, and the _____, the _____/ _____, the _____/ _____ and the _____ _____.

7. The early music written for the Mass is known as plain-chant or _____ _____.

8. This early music was notated in symbols called _____.

9. Early music was built on a type of musical scale called a(n) _____, which were of two types, the _____ _____ and the _____.

10. The Mediaeval singing style which involved the use of a large number of notes for each syllable of text is known as _____.

11. The Mediaeval singing style which involved the use of only one note per syllable is known as _____.

12. A Mass for the Dead is usually referred to as a _____ _____ _____.

13. The two principal groups of secular musicians in the Middle Ages were the _____ in Southern France, and the _____ in Northern France.

14. The earliest polyphony in the Middle Ages seems to have been created by adding a second voice part to chant, a process known as _____.

15. In early two-part music, the original voice (usually based on chant) was called the _____, and the second voice was identified as the _____.

16. The first major musical center of the Middle Ages was Paris and its leading composer, the choirmaster of the Notre Dame Cathedral, _____.

17. The above composer's major collection of music is entitled the _____ _____ _____.

18. The next major composer of this period was _____, who edited, revised and added to his predecessor's works.

19. A major type of composition during this period was the _____.

20. The music of the Fourteenth Century was known as the
    _____ _____, a term coined by the com-
    poser _____ _____ _____.

21. The principal composer of the French Ars Nova was _____
    _____.

22. The first complete polyphonic setting of the Ordinary of
    the Mass was Machaut's _____.

23. Four popular music forms of secular music of the French
    Ars Nova were the _____, _____, _____
    and _____.

24. Three important music forms of secular music of the
    Italian Ars Nova were the _____, _____
    nd _____.

25. The principal composer of the Italian Ars Nova was _____
    _____.

LIST THE FIVE PARTS OF THE MASS WHICH WERE MOST
OFTEN SET TO MUSIC IN THE PROPER ORDER OF THEIR
OCCURRENCE IN THE MASS

AGNUS DEI, CREDO, KYRIE ELEISON, SANCTUS, GLORIA

   1. _____
   2. _____
   3. _____
   4. _____
   5. _____

INDICATE THE FINAL FOR EACH OF THE FOLLOWING MODES:

   1. _____ Hypodorian
   2. _____ Lydian
   3. _____ Hypomixolydian
   4. _____ Dorian
   5. _____ Phrygian
   6. _____ Mixolydian
   7. _____ Hypolydian
   8. _____ Hypophrygian

LISTENING STUDY GUIDE

LISTEN TO EACH OF THE INDICATED MUSIC EXAMPLES
AND ANSWER THE FOLLOWING QUESTIONS:

EXAMPLE 1:   REQUIEM MASS: INTROIT
             SIDE 2, BAND 1
   (1) The melodic range is:
       (a) Narrow
       (b) Wide
   (2) The texture is:
       (a) Homophonic
       (b) Monophonic
   (3) The relationship of text to melody is:
       (a) Melismatic
       (b) Syllabic
   (4) The melody is:
       (a) Conjunct
       (b) Disjunct
   (5) The rhythm is:
       (a) Strict
       (b) Free

EXAMPLE 2:   LE CHATELAIN: LE NOVIAUS TENS
                            SIDE 2, BAND 2
   (1) The texture is:
       (a) Monophonic
       (b) Homophonic
   (2) The text is:
       (a) Sacred
       (b) Secular
   (3) The meter is:
       (a) Duple
       (b) Triple
   (4) The melodic range is:
       (a) Narrow
       (b) Wide
   (5) The singer is:
       (a) Male
       (b) Female

EXAMPLE 3:   LEONIN: VIDERUNT OMNES
                      SIDE 2, BAND 3
   (1) The melody is:
       (a) Conjunct
       (b) Disjunct
   (2) The text setting is:
       (a) Syllabic
       (b) Melismatic
   (3) How many voice parts are there?
       (a) Two
       (b) Three

22

(4) At the beginning, the lower voice or tenor moves:
    (a) In a series of long, drawn-out notes
    (b) In exact duplication with the upper voice
(5) The closing section is:
    (a) Monophonic
    (b) Polyphonic

EXAMPLE 4: MACHAUT: <u>DOUCE DAME JOLIE</u>
                                    SIDE 2, BAND 4
(1) The texture is:
    (a) Monophonic
    (b) Homophonic
(2) The meter is:
    (a) Duple
    (b) Triple
(3) The timbre is:
    (a) Vocal
    (b) Instrumental
    (c) Vocal and instrumental
(4) The rhythm is:
    (a) Free
    (b) Pronounced
(5) The song is organized into:
    (a) Four sections without repetition
    (b) Two sections repeated in a certain pattern

CHAPTER 7

Renaissance Music

<u>KEY TERMS AND CONCEPTS</u>
<u>IMPORTANT COMPOSERS</u>

A. GENERAL CHARACTERISTICS OF RENAISSANCE MUSIC
B. NEW DEVELOPMENTS IN POLYPHONY
    1. Four-Part Texture
    2. Careful use of dissonance
    3. Wide use of imitation
    4. Text painting
C. RELIGIOUS MUSIC
    1. Fifteenth century motet
    2. Use of canons
    3. Paraphrase technique
    4. Reformation music
        a. The Chorale
D. SECULAR MUSIC
    1. Italian
        a. Frottola
        b. Madrigal
    2. French
        a. Chanson
    3. English
        a. Madrigal
        b. Ayre
        c. Lute song
        d. Ballett
E. INSTRUMENTAL MUSIC
    1. Consorts of instruments
        a. Broken consorts
    2. Instruments
        a. String: Viol, Lute, Gamba
        b. Wind: Recorder, Shawm, Sackbut

                c. Keyboard: Organ, Harpsichord
        3. Instrumental Dances
                a. Pavane
                b. Galliard
        4. Instrumental Forms
                a. Ricercar
                b. Fantasia
                c. Canzona
    F. IMPORTANT RENAISSANCE COMPOSERS
        1. Guillaume Dufey (c. 1410-1474)
        2. Johannes Ockeghem (c. 1410-c. 1497)
        3. Josquin des Prez (c. 1410-1497)
        4. Giovanni Pierluigi da Palestrina (c. 1524-1594)
        5. Roland de Lassus (1532-1594)
        6. William Byrd (1543-1623)
        7. Carlo Gesualdo (1560-1613)
        8. Claudio Montevardi (1567-1643)
        9. Thomas Morley (1557-1602)
       10. John Dowland (1562-1626)
    G. MUSIC PRINTING
        1. Petrucci
        2. 1501
        3. Odhecaton
        4. Venice

COMPLETE THE FOLLOWING:

1. The Renaissance period first began in that part of Europe
    known today as _____.

2. Renaissance musical styles evolved from the works of com-
    posers in Burgundy and _____.

3. The Renaissance period covers the last half of the _____
    century and the entire _____ century.

4. By the mid-Renaissance, _____ parts had
    become the normal number for a polyphonic work.

5. One of the major elements of Renaissance polyphony was
    _____.

6. Renaissance composers were much more careful in their use
    of _____ than were Mediaeval composers.

7. A common Renaissance compositional technique in setting
    words to music was known as _____ _____.

8. One of the earliest important composers of the early
    Renaissance, who came from Cambrai, in northern France,
    was _____.

9. The leading composer of the next generation, who came from the Netherlands, was _____.

10. The Renaissance composer who was one of the first truly great composers of music history was _____.

11. The Renaissance composer who was born in Flanders, made his name in Florence, and eventually was attached to the Imperial Court in Vienna was _____.

12. The principal Protestant figure of the Reformation, a man well-versed in music and aware of its importance in religion was _____.

13. The principal musical form of the Reformation was the _____.

14. In order to deal with the Reformation, the Catholic Church set in motion a Counter-Reformation at an extended Church Council in the Northern Italian city of _____.

15. One of the most celebrated composers of the late Renaissance, often referred to as "The Divine Roland" was the composer _____, also known by the Italian version of his name _____.

16. The leading Italian composer of the late Renaissance, who was responsible for a rebirth of Catholic Church music following the Reformation, was _____.

17. One of the leading cities of the late Renaissance period was Venice, and two of its principal composers were uncle and nephew, Andrea and Giovanni _____.

18. England became a Protestant nation during the Renaissance but one of its leading composers, who wrote both Catholic and Protestant music during this period was _____.

19. Music printing began in the year _____ in the city of _____, with a collection of music entitled the _____, issued by a man named _____.

20. One of the most popular secular vocal forms of the late Renaissance, particularly in Italy and England was the _____.

21. One of the most avant-garde and colorful composers of Italian madrigals was _____.

22. Another major composer of Italian madrigals, a composer who would become a principal composer of opera in the

early eighteenth century. was _____.

23. A leading Renaissance composer of madrigals in England was _____.

24. A group of instruments during the Renaissance period was known as a _____, and a favorite dance form for instruments was a pair of dances, the _____ and the _____.

25. Two important Renaissance keyboard instruments were the organ and the _____.

INDICATE WHICH OF THE FOLLOWING MUSICAL STYLES IS MORE COMMON DURING THE MEDIAEVAL (M) OR THE RENAISSANCE (R) PERIODS

1. _____ Narrow range of melody.
2. _____ More music written specifically for instruments.
3. _____ Freer use of dissonance.
4. _____ Polyphonic music sung by soloists.
5. _____ Polyphonic music sung by small choirs.
6. _____ Complex rhythmic structure.
7. _____ Polyphonic music for four voices the norm.
8. ._____ Monophony very important texture.
9. _____ Freer, imitative musical forms.
10. _____ Instrumental pieces other than dances.

WHO WROTE EACH OF THE FOLLOWING COMPOSITIONS:

1. Absalom, fili mi   _____
2. Choralis Constantinus   _____
3. A Mighty Fortress   _____
4. Si ch'io vorrei morire   _____
5. Now is the Month of Maying _____

LISTENING STUDY GUIDE

LISTEN TO EACH OF THE INDICATED EXAMPLES
AND ANSWER THE FOLLOWING QUESTIONS:

EXAMPLE 1: JOSQUIN: ABSALON FILI MI
                      SIDE2, BAND 5
    1. The opening phrase is:
        a. Imitative
        b. Homophonic
    2. How many voice parts are heard?
        a. Three
        b. Four

27

3. The singers are:
   a. Men
   b. Women
   c. Men and Women
4. The music is:
   a. Accompanied
   b. Unaccompanied
5. The meter is:
   a. Duple
   b. Triple

EXAMPLE 2: PALESTRINA: MISSA BREVIS: KYRIE: SIDE 2, BAND 6
1. The opening phrase is:
   a. Imitative
   b. Homophonic
2. How many sections are there?
   a. Two
   b. Three
   c. Four
3. The melodic line is:
   a. Conjunct
   b. Disjunct
4. How many voice parts are heard?
   a. Two
   b. Three
   c. Four
5. The music is:
   a. Accompanied
   b. Unaccompanied

EXAMPLE 3: MONTEVERDI: SI CH'IO VORREI MORIRE: SIDE2, BAND 7
1. The texture of the opening phrase is:
   a. Polyphonic
   b. Homophonic
2. How many voice parts are heard?
   a. Three
   b. Four
   c. Five
3. The language being sung is:
   a. Italian
   b. Latin
4. The madrigal begins with:
   a. A major triad
   b. A dissonant chord
5. The music is:
   a. Accompanied
   b. Unaccompanied

EXAMPLE 4: MORLEY: <u>NOW IS THE MONTH OF MAYING</u>:
<u>SIDE 2, BAND 8</u>

1. How many sections are there?
    a. Two
    b. Three
    c. Four
2. How many voices are heard?
    a. Three
    b. Four
    c. Five
3. For the most part, the voices move:
    a. In a complex contrapuntal texture
    b. Together, in a chordal texture
4. The texture is:
    a. Homophonic
    b. Polyphonic
5. A unique feature of the chorus is:
    a. Added voices
    b. Fa-la-la refrain

CHAPTER 8

Introduction to Baroque Musical Style

                    a. Organ
                    b. Harpsichord
                    c. Clavichord
                3. Wind Instruments
                    a. Flute, Oboe, Bassoon
                    b. Trumpet, horn, trombone
                4. Beginning of the orchestra
        E. TYPES OF COMPOSITION AND FORM
                1. Vocal works
                    a. Opera, cantata, oratorio
                2. Instrumental works
                    a. Sonata, concerto, suite, fugue
                3. Multi-movement works
        F. CONTRAST AND THE CONCERTATO STYLE
                1. Treble-bass polarity
                2. Terraced dynamics
                3. Rhythmic and metric contrast
        G. COLONIAL AMERICAN MUSIC
                1. Early Religious Music
                    a. Ainsworth Psalter
                2. "Usual" vs. "Regular" singing

COMPLETE THE FOLLOWING:

1. The term "Baroque" may have its origins as a word for a
    misshapen pearl, in the _____ language, or
    from a term relating to a far-fetched syllogistic argument
    in the _____ language, or may even derive
    from the name of an Italian painter, Federigo _____.

2. At first the Baroque era was considered to be a period of
    artistic _____, although now it is con-
    sidered to be a period of great creative genius.

3. The Baroque period marked the growth of absolute mon-
    archies and the leading example of the absolute monarch
    was Louis XIV of _____, often called the
    "_____ King."

4. Two leading painters of the Baroque Era were _____
    _____ and _____.

5. The overt emotionalism expressed in much music of the
    Baroque Era is known as the "Doctrine of the _____
    _____."

6. An important group in the City of Florence which was
    interested in reviving ancient Greek drama, and eventu-
    ally wound up inventing opera, was called the _____
    and met at the home of Count _____.

7. The theatrical style which emerged at the beginning of the Baroque Era, in which the music was subordinate to the text was known in Italy as the _____ _____.

8. The Baroque concept of a principal melody supported by a simple chordal accompaniment was known as _____.

9. Typical of the early Baroque vocal style was the creation of greater affective expression through the use of elaborate melodic embellishments called _____.

10. Two different kinds of vocal compositions which emerged during the early Baroque, and which became integral parts of the basic structure of opera were the _____, which emphasized musical declamation, and the _____, which featured elaborate melodies, often ornamental.

11. A vocal style of the early Baroque Era which deemphasized ornamentation in favor of lyrical melodies was known as _____.

12. A vocal form which was more melodic than recitative, but less rhythmic than the aria, was known as a(n) _____ _____.

13. A prominent feature of the Baroque style was the use of a melodic fragment repeated on successively higher or lower pitches, a device known as _____.

14. The old modality of earlier periods of music was rapidly being replaced during the Baroque Era by the development of major-minor _____.

15. The harmonic technique of one chord leading to another during the progress of the music, is known as chordal _____.

16. A new system of tuning which emerged during the Baroque Era was known as _____ _____.

17. Baroque music is essentially comprised of two basic elements, a melody line, often highly embellished, and a bass line, which came to be known as _____ _____.

18. Beneath the base line of Baroque Music, a kind of "musical shorthand," known as _____ _____ was written to indicate to the accompanist (usually a keyboardist, what chords to play over the bass line, a technique known as _____.

19. The Baroque style in which the same theme is repeated by different voices, either exactly or with imitations, is known as _____ _____.

20. The major keyboard instruments of the Baroque Era were the _____, the _____, and the _____.

21. During the Baroque Era the instrumental group known as the _____ made its first appearance.

22. Many musical compositions of the Baroque Era were comprised of several larger independent, but interdependent parts, known as _____.

23. The element of contrast, which is basic to Baroque musical style, is known as the _____ style.

24. The element of contrast is evident in the dynamic levels of Baroque music, in which a loud section is followed by a soft section, or a soft section is followed by a loud section, a technique known as _____ dynamics.

25. The Colonial Americans sang mostly sacred songs from a book of rhymed, metrical psalms called a _____, either in an untrained manner known as _____ singing or in a trained manner, known as _____ singing.

LIST THE THREE PRINCIPAL INSTRUMENTS OF THE BAROQUE ERA IN EACH OF THE FOLLOWING CATEGORIES

STRING   WOODWIND   BRASS

_____   _____   _____
_____   _____   _____
_____   _____   _____

INDICATE WHICH OF THE FOLLOWING STYLES IS RENAISSANCE (R) AND WHICH IS BAROQUE (B)

1. _____ Conjunct, singable melodies.
2. _____ Instrumental music more important than before.
3. _____ Much use of sequence.
4. _____ Harmony based on church modes.
5. _____ Imitative forms.
6. _____ Multi-movement works.
7. _____ Rise of opera.
8. _____ Ornamented melodic lines.
9. _____ Careful control of dissonance.
10. _____ Steady, driving rhythm.

CHAPTER 9

Baroque Vocal Music

<u>KEY TERMS AND CONCEPTS</u>
<u>IMPORTANT COMPOSERS</u>

A. GENERAL TRENDS IN VOCAL MUSIC
   1. Monody
   2. Stile Rappresentativo
   3. Continuo madrigal
B. OPERA
   1. Recitatives
      a. Secco
      b. Accompagnato
   2. Arias
      a. Strophic-bass aria
      b. Ostinato aria
      c. Da capo aria
   3. Castrato singer
   4. Venetian opera
      a. First public opera house (1617)
   5. Neapolitan opera
      a. Homophonic, melody-dominated style
      b. Opera buffa
   6. French opera
      a. Fewer, shorter arias
      b. Importance of visual aspect
      c. More colorful orchestration
   7. English opera
      a. Masque
      b. Choral emphasis
C. CANTATA
   1. Italian secular cantata
   2. German sacred cantata

D. ORATORIO
  1. Laude
  2. Italian, German, English
E. MASS
  1. Missa Brevis
F. IMPORTANT BAROQUE COMPOSERS OF VOCAL MUSIC
  1. Giulio Caccini (1546-1618)
     a. Euridice, Le Nuove Musiche
  2. Claudio Monteverdi (1567-1643)
     a. Orfeo
  3. Alessandro Scarlatti (1660-1725)
  4. Jean-Baptiste Lully (1632-1687)
  5. Henry Purcell (1659-1695)
     a. Dido and Aeneas
  6. Georg Friedrich Handel (1685-1759)
     a. Julius Caesar, Messiah
  7. Heinrich Schuetz (1585-1672)
  8. Dietrich Buxtehude (c. 1637-1717)
  9. Johann Sebastian Bach (1685-1750)
     a. B Minor Mass

COMPLETE THE FOLLOWING:

1. One of the earliest Baroque composers of monody was the Italian composer _____, who co-authored one of the earliest operas.

2. A major treatise of the above composer, a document which has become a major source of information on early monody is his publication entitled _____.

3. A type of madrigal of the early Baroque, in which the polarization of bass and _____ occurs, is known as a(n) _____ madrigal.

4. The first major vocal form of the early Baroque Era was the _____, and the first great masterpiece in this new form was Monteverdi's _____.

5. A stylistic trait of some early Baroque vocal music was the inclusion of notes not part of the scale, an aspect known as _____.

6. Of the two principal types of recitative in early opera, one had only a simple continuo accompaniment, and was known as _____, and the other featured an accompaniment of a larger instrumental ensemble, and was known as _____.

7. The most popular type of aria in the early days of opera was the _____ aria.

8. Opera began in Florence, but the first city to build the first opera house, in the year _____, was the city of _____.

9. Another major opera center of the early Baroque was Naples, and the leading composer of Neapolitan opera was Allesandro _____.

10. In Naples, comic opera made its first appearance, a type of opera called by the Italians _____.

11. The leading French composer of opera during the early Baroque was _____.

12. The leading English composer of opera during the early Baroque was _____, whose major opera was _____.

13. A German-born composer, who was trained in Italy, but who spent most of his creative life in England was _____ _____, one of whose important operas was _____ _____.

14. Since women were not allowed to perform publicly during this period, the soprano and alto parts were sung by surgically-altered male singers known as _____.

15. Another early Baroque vocal form which originally indicated simply a piece for voices, but which later took on a very specific form and structure, was the _____ _____.

16. The leading Italian composer of the above form was Allesandro _____, and the leading German composers of this form were _____ and _____.

17. The great German choral composer of the late Baroque Era was one of the most famous composer of all times, _____ _____.

18. A major vocal form of the Baroque Era, which was created to fill the gaps during Lent, when opera houses were closed was the _____.

19. The composer who established the above form was the Italian composer _____, but the great master of the form was the German/English composer _____ _____, whose major work in this form is the great masterpiece.

20. Catholic masses continued to be wri-ten during the Baroque Era, including shorter masses, known as _____

and masses of enormous proportion, like the great B-Minor
_____, and the great _____ Mass
by the great master composer Johann Sebastian _____.

WHO WROTE THE FOLLOWING BAROQUE VOCAL WORKS?

1. Messiah   _____
2. Orfeo   _____
3. Julius Caesar   _____
4. Dido and Aeneas   _____
5. Cantiones Sacrae   _____

LISTENING STUDY GUIDE

LISTEN TO EACH OF THE INDICATED MUSIC EXAMPLES
AND ANSWER THE FOLLOWING QUESTIONS:

EXAMPLE 1: MONTEVERDI: ORFEO: TU SE MORTA
SIDE 2, Band 9
1. The accompanying instrument is a(n):
   a. Organ
   b. Harpsichord
2. The singer is a:
   a. Bass
   b. Tenor
3. The style is:
   a. Polyphonic
   b. Monodic
4. The language is:
   a. Italian
   b. Latin
5. The mood of the piece is:
   a. Light
   b. Serious

EXAMPLE @: BACH: CANTATA #80
SIDE3, BAND 1
1. How many voice parts are heard?
   a. Three
   b. Four
2. The texture is:
   a. Homophonic
   b. Polyphonic
3. A prominent brass instrument heard is the:
   a. Trombone
   b. Trumpet
4. The tonality is primarily:
   a. Major
   b. Minor

5. The most prominent textural aspect is:
    a. Chordal
    b. Imitative

EXAMPLE 3: HANDEL: MESSIAH: FOR UNTO US A CHILD IS BORN
                          SIDE 3, BAND 2
    1. The opening measures are:
        a. Choral
        b. Instrumental
    2. The two opening voices are:
        a. Soprano and tenor
        b. Alto and bass

    3. The style of singing is frequently:
        a. Melismatic
        b. Syllabic
    4. The texture at the words "Wonderful! Counsellor!" is:
        a. Polyphonic
        b. Homophonic
    5. A prominent textural aspect of this piece is:
        a. Imitation
        b. Monody

EXAMPLE 4: BACH: B-MINOR MASS: SANCTUS
                        SIDE 3, BAND 3
    1. Instruments prominently heard at the beginning are:
        a. Brasses
        b. Woodwinds
    2. The vocal treatment of the word "Sanctus" is both:
        a. Syllabic and melismatic
        b. Monodic and monophonic
    3. The setting of the text "Pleni sunt coeli" is:
        a. Homophonic
        b. Contrapuntal
    4. The orchestral accompaniment is:
        a. Secondary to the vocal parts
        b. An equal partner to the vocal parts
    5. How many voice parts are heard?
        a. Six
        b. Eight
        c. Six and eight

CHAPTER 10

Baroque Instrumental Music

                b. Suites for ensembles
                    1. Combination of slow and fast dances
                c. Partita
            4. Toccata
                a. Keyboard, especially organ
        G. IMPORTANT BAROQUE COMPOSERS OF INSTRUMENTAL MUSIC
            1. Arcangelo Corelli (1653-1713)
            2. Francois Couperin (1668-1733)
            3. Domenico Scarletti (1685-1757)
            4. Jean-Baptiste Lully (1632-1687)
            5. Giuseppe Torelli (1658-1709)
            6. Antonio Vivaldi (c. 1675-1741)
                a. Four Seasons
            7. Johann Sebastian Bach (1685-1750)
                a. The Art of the Fugue
            8. Girolomo Frescobaldi (1583-1643)

COMPLETE THE FOLLOWING:

1. The single most important legacy of the Baroque Era was
    the development of _____ and the rise of
    _____ music.

2. The two most important sonata forms of the Baroque Era
    were the _____ sonata, written for one instru-
    ment and basso continuo, and the _____ sonata,
    written for two solo instruments and basso continuo.

3. Of the latter of the two sonata forms above, there are
    two types, the _____ sonata and the _____
    sonata.

4. The leading composer of trio sonatas during the late 17th
    Century was the Italian composer _____.

5. A major composer of solo sonatas during the late Baroque
    was the Italian/Spanish composer Domenico _____,
    who wrote more than 600 sonatas for _____.

6. The first orchestra of the Baroque Era was established in
    _____, by the composer _____.

7. The principal orchestral form of the Baroque era was the
    _____ _____, which was comprised of two
    parts, the solo section, called the _____,
    and the larger orchestral section called the _____
    _____.

8. The concerto form for a single instrument with orchestral
    accompaniment, the _____ concerto, was
    pioneered by the Italian composer _____.

9. The concerto form in which the opening theme recurs throughout the concerto, is known as _____ form.

10. The musical term for "work," or "composition" is _____ _____.

11. More than 450 solo concertos were written by the late Baroque composer _____ who was active in the City of _____.

12. The most mature form of imitative counterpoint is the _____ which features a principal theme, or melody, known as the _____ and intervening sections known as _____.

13. The unchallenged master of the above contrapultal form was _____, whose final work is a monumental collection of such works (left unfinished at his death), which he called _____.

14. A major work of Bach, which contains a pair of preludes and fugues in every major and minor key, and which became a major work in the establishment of tonality is the _____.

15. The orchestral introductions or interludes written for vocal works such as operas or cantatas during the Baroque Era were known as _____.

16. There were two types of opera overtures during the Baroque Era, the French overture, pioneered by _____ and the Italian overture, pioneered by _____.

17. The Baroque composition consisting of a number of movements, each like a dance and all in the same, or related, keys, is called a(n) _____.

18. The above form was called a(n) _____ in France, and its principal composer in that country was the great harpsichord composer _____.

19. Another name for the above form, a title occasionally used by J. S. Bach, is the _____.

20. A virtuosic instrumental form, a kind of prelude, which was originally written for keyboard instruments to demonstrate the skill of the performer was the _____, and one of the major composers in this form was the Italian composer _____.

41

LIST THE FOLLOWING INSTRUMENTS
OF A STANDARD BAROQUE ORCHESTRA

1. The three principal types of string instruments:

    _____
    _____
    _____

2. The three principal types of wind instruments (pairs):

    _____
    _____
    _____

3. Three possible continuo harmony instruments:

    _____
    _____
    _____

4. Three possible continuo bass instruments:

    _____
    _____
    _____

LISTENING STUDY GUIDE

LISTEN TO EACH OF THE INDICATED MUSIC EXAMPLE
AND ANSWER THE FOLLOWING QUESTIONS:

EXAMPLE 1: SCARLATTI: SONATA IN C MAJOR, K.159:
                              SIDE 3, BAND 6
1. The performing instrument is a:
    a. Piano
    b. Harpsichord
2. How many sections comprise this sonata?
    a. Two
    b. Three
3. The harmony is primarily:
    a. Major
    b. Minor
4. The texture is:
    a. Polyphonic
    b. Homophonic
5. Many repeated notes are heard.
    a. True
    b. False

42

EXAMPLE 2: VIVALDI: <u>WINTER CONCERTO</u>
<u>SIDE 3, BAND 4</u>

1. The tempo of the music is probably:
    a. Allegro
    b. Adagio
2. A prominent compositional technique used is:
    a. Melismatic writing
    b. Sequence
3. The solo violin moves mainly in:
    a. Long, sustained tones
    b. Rapid tones
4. The meter is:
    a. Duple
    b. Triple
5. The tonality is prominently:
    a. Major
    b. Minor

EXAMPLE 3: HANDEL: <u>CONCERTO IN Bb MAJOR, OPUS 3, #1</u>
<u>SIDE 3, BAND 5</u>

1. The solo group is comprised of a violin and two:
    a. Clarinets
    b. Oboes
2. The returning principal theme is called a:
    a. Recapitulation
    b. Ritornello
3. The opening theme is comprised of two:
    a. Chords
    b. Arpeggios
4. A prominent compositional technique used is:
    a. Sequence
    b. Monody
5. The tempo is probably:
    a. Andante
    b. Allegro

EXAMPLE 4: BACH: <u>FUGUE IN G MINOR</u>
<u>SIDE 3, BAND 7</u>

1. The performing instrument is a(n):
    a. Harpsichord
    b. Organ
2. The texture is primarily:
    a. Homophonic
    b. Contrapuntal
3. During the exposition, or first section:
    a. Each voice presents the subject once.
    b. The first voice is dominant throughout.
4. In the middle section, the subject is presented:
    a. Three times
    b. Four times

5. The tonality is:
    a. Major
    b. Minor

CHAPTER 11

Introduction to the Musical Style of the Classical Era

KEY TERMS AND CONCEPTS

A. THE EMERGENCE OF THE CLASSICAL STYLE IN MUSIC
    1. Rococo Style
    2. Empfindsamer Stil
B. THE CLASSICAL-ROMANTIC CONTINUUM
    1. Classical Order
    2. Romantic Subjectivism
C. MELODY AND RHYTHM
    1. Emphasis on melody
    2. Regular phrase structure
    3. Rhythmic variety
D. HARMONY AND TEXTURE
    1. Major-Minor harmony
    2. Use of modulation
    3. Keys are related
        a. Relative minors and majors
    4. Increased homophonic texture
        a. Some contrapuntal texture
E. TIMBRE AND DYNAMICS
    1. Enlarged, improved orchestra
    2. Pianoforte (piano) replaces harpsichord.
    3. Increased use of crescendo, decrescendo.
F. TYPES OF COMPOSITIONS AND FORM
    1. Vocal Music
        a. Operas, songs
        b. Masses, oratorios
    2. Instrumental Music
        a. Sonata cycle
            (1) Three or four movements, each in a
                different form

           (2) Solo Sonatas, String Quartets
           (3) Symphonies, Concertos
      3. Sonata Form
          a. Exposition
          b. Development
          c. Recapitulation
          d. May begin with an Introduction
          e. May close with a Coda
      4. Rondo Form
          a. ABACA
      5. Sonata-Rondo Form
      6. Binary, Ternary Form
      7. Theme and Variations Form
  G. MUSIC IN 18TH CENTURY AMERICA
      1. Singing Schools
          a. Fasola singing
          b. Shape-note Notation
      2. Secular folk music influence
      3. Influence of European music

COMPLETE THE FOLLOWING:

1. The classical period of music history falls within the
    late _____ and early _____ centuries.

2. During this period, a preference for classic _____
    in both art and music emerged.

3. Two leading composers of the early classical style were
    both sons of the great Baroque composer _____.

4. A pre-Classical style which emphasized ornamental, pretty
    and pleasantly artificial music was the _____
    style, a leading composer of which was the French com-
    poser _____.

5. A pre-Classical style which allowed for sensitivity and
    the expression of a variety of moods was the _____
    style, a leading composer of which was _____.

6. In the late eighteenth century, _____ took a
    dominant role in both vocal and instrumental music.

7. A major aspect of the Classical style is that the music
    is organized into regularly recurring _____.

8. Classical music allows for much more rhythmic _____
    than did Baroque music.

9. The structural basis of Classical music is _____.

10. In the Classical style, the _____ chord intro-
    duces tension, which is resolved with the _____
    chord.

11. Modulation in Classical music is usually to _____
    _____ keys (such as V and IV) or to the relative
    _____ or _____ key.

12. The texture of Classical music is usually _____.

13. The Classical orchestra was comprised of _____ to _____
    players, and was dominated by the _____
    section.

14. The leading orchestra of the Classical Era was in the
    City of _____, and was led by _____.

15. In the seating arrangement of a Classical orchestra, the
    violins usually set on the conductor's _____
    and the cellos on the conductor's _____, as
    today.

16. The most common musical form of the Classical Era was the
    _____ _____ which could be
    found in the _____ for piano, the _____
    for orchestra, and the _____ for soloists and
    orchestra.

17. The three basic parts of sonata form were the _____
    _____, _____, and the _____
    _____.

18. Occasionally a short section called the _____
    was added to the end of a piece of music in sonata form.

19. A popular Classical form which involves the recurrence of
    a principal theme with the interspersion of two or more
    secondary themes, was the _____ form.

20. The two basic forms of the Classical Era were the binary
    and _____ forms.

21. Another popular form of the Classical Era was the theme
    and _____ form.

22. In Colonial America, during the Classical Era, an impor-
    tant musical institution was the _____ school.

23. A leading composer in Colonial America was the former
    tanner and self-taught musician, William _____.

24. A unique singing and teaching method in Colonial America was the _____ system, which used a new system of music notation called the _____ system.

25. Three leading Colonial American amateur musicians were Thomas Jefferson, Benjamin Franklin, and Francis _____ _____, the latter of whom was one of America's first writers of secular songs, including _____ _____.

ANSWER THE FOLLOWING QUESTIONS ABOUT THE EIGHTEENTH-CENTURY ORCHESTRA

1. What type of instrument dominates the orchestra?
   _____

2. What are the principal double-reed instruments of the orchestra?
   _____
   _____
   _____

3. What single-reed instrument was added late in the 18th Century?
   _____

4. Which brass instruments were part of the Classical orchestra?
   _____
   _____

5. What was the only percussion instrument in the Classical orchestra?
   _____

INDICATE WHICH OF THE FOLLOWING ELEMENTS IS ESSENTIALLY A BAROQUE (B) CONCEPT AND WHICH IS ESSENTIALLY A CLASSICAL ERA CONCEPT (C)

1. _____ Melodies built on motives and short phrases.
2. _____ Polyphonic texture, often imitative.
3. _____ Frequent ornamentation.
4. _____ Instrumental music more prominent than vocal.
5. _____ Greater rhythmic variety.

CHAPTER 12

Symphonies of Haydn and Mozart

KEY TERMS, CONCEPTS AND IMPORTANT NAMES AND TITLES

A. DEVELOPMENT OF THE CLASSICAL SYMPHONY
    1. Antecedents of the symphony
        a. Italian Overture (Fast-Slow-Fast)
        b. Baroque Suite (Independent movements)
    2. Structure of the symphony
        a. Three, then four movements
        b. Tempo: fast, slow, moderate, fast
        c. First movement usually in sonata form
        d. Second movement in binary or sonata form
            (1) Occasionally theme and variations form
        e. Third movement usually a minuet, with trio, in ternary (ABA) form
        f. Fourth movement in sonata or rondo form
            (1) Occasionally in sonata-rondo form
        g. Concept of dramatic development from within
B. HAYDN'S SYMPHONIES
    1. 104 Symphonies
    2. The London Symphonies
        a. #94, the "Surprise" Symphony
    3. The Patronage System
        a. Haydn's patrons, the Esterhazys
C. MOZART'S SYMPHONIES
    1. 41 Symphonies
    2. Köchel numbering system
    3. No patron
    4. The final symphonic trilogy
        a. Symphonies #39, 40 and 41.
            (1) #41 known as the "Jupiter" symphony

COMPLETE THE FOLLOWING:

1. The fast-slow-fast structure of the early symphony was influenced by the three-part _____ _____.

2. The concept of independent movements in the symphony derives from the concept of the Baroque _____.

3. A dance form which was added to the symphonic form in the 18th Century was the _____.

4. The first major composer of symphonies was _____.

5. The standard length of the symphony was _____ movements, with tempos which were, in order, _____, moderate and _____, respectfully.

6. Haydn's patrons were the Hungarian aristocratic family named _____, for whom Haydn was little more than a skilled _____, as part of a system known as _____.

7. Haydn wrote _____ symphonies.

8. Haydn's last twelve symphonies are known as the _____ _____, or _____ symphonies, after the orchestra for which they were written, and the impressario who commissioned them.

9. Haydn's 94th Symphony is known as the _____ symphony, because of an unexpected loud chord in the second movement.

10. Mozart, one of music's most brilliant child prodigies, was first taught by his _____.

11. Mozart, like Haydn, was of what nationality? _____ _____.

12. In addition to his 41+ symphonies, Mozard wrote _____ piano concertos and _____ violin concertos.

13. Mozart's works were organized and catalogued by the Austrian musicographer _____.

14. Unlike Haydn, who worked out his musical ideas very laboriously, Mozart composed _____.

15. Mozart's last three symphonies, perhaps his greatest works in this genre, were written within the space of _____ weeks.

LISTENING STUDY GUIDE

LISTEN TO EACH OF THE INDICATED MUSIC EXAMPLES AND ANSWER THE FOLLOWING QUESTIONS:

EXAMPLE 1:   HAYDN: SYMPHONY #94 ("SURPRISE" SYMPHONY)
FIRST MOVEMENT
SIDE 4, BAND 1

1.   The first movement begins with:
    a.   Loud, crashing chords
    b.   A slow introduction
2.   The principal theme is:
    a.   Dancelike
    b.   Meditative
3.   The tonality is primarily:
    a.   Major
    b.   Minor
4.   Which theme is more lyrical?
    a.   First
    b.   Second
5.   Which of the following is probably the meter of the main part of this movement?
    a.   Four-four
    b.   Six-eight

EXAMPLE 2:   HAYDN: SYMPHONY #94 ("SURPRISE" SYMPHONY):
SECOND MOVEMENT
SIDE 4, BAND 1

1.   The Theme of this movement spells out a:
    a.   Major triad
    b.   Diminished chord
2.   The form of this movement is:
    a.   Sonata
    b.   Theme and Variations
3.   The "surprise" of the movement is:
    a.   A sudden change of key
    b.   A sudden loud chord
4.   The movement is entirely in the major key.
    a.   True
    b.   False
5.   What is the probable tempo of this movement?
    a.   Allegro
    b.   Andante

EXAMPLE 3:   MOZART: SYMPHONY #40:   FIRST MOVEMENT
SIDE 4, BAND 3

1.   The opening motive of this movement contains how many notes?
    a. Five
    b.   Three
2.   Which of the two themes of this movement is more lyrical?

          a. First
          b. Second
   3. The second theme is primarily:
          a. Conjunct
          b. Disjunct
   4. The tempo of this movement is probably:
          a. Andante
          b. Allegro
   5. The second theme is in what mode?
          a. Major
          b. Minor

EXAMPLE 4: MOZART: SYMPHONY #40: THIRD MOVEMENT
                        SIDE 4, BAND 4
   1. The meter of this movement is:
          a. Duple
          b. Triple
   2. The direction of the melodic line of the first theme
      is:
          a. Rising
          b. Falling
   3. How many parts does this movement have?
          a. Three
          b. Four
   4. The trio section is in what mode?
          a. Major
          b. Minor
   5. Which theme is the most lyrical?
          a. First
          b. Second

CHAPTER 13

Symphonies of Beethoven

A. THE MUSICIAN IN AN AGE OF REVOLUTION
   1. Beethoven lived as an independent composer
   2. The musician now enjoyed a higher social status than under the patronage system
B. BEETHOVEN'S SYMPHONIES
   1. Nine symphonies
      a. #1, #2, #4, & #18 are classical in style
      b. #3, #5, #6 & #7 are romantic in style
      c. #9 breaks with symphonic traditions by adding voices to the symphony
   2. Symphonies are longer
      a. Longer introductions, codas
      b. Longer, more complex development sections
      c. Sixth symphony has five movements
   3. Larger orchestra, additional instruments
      a. Trombones added
   4. Use of shorter melodic themes (motives)
      a. Single motivic idea in successive movements
   5. Use of scherzo as third movement
   6. Programmatic writing
      a. Sixth Symphony, "Pastoral"
   7. Third Symphony ("Eroica")
      a. Originally dedicated to Napoleon
      b. First truly Romantic symphony
   8. Fifth Symphony
      a. Probably the best-known symphony
C. BEETHOVEN'S DEAFNESS

COMPLETE THE FOLLOWING:

1. Beethoven grew up in the German city of _____,
    but spent most of his life in the Austrian city of
    _____.

2. Although known as a pianist, Beethoven began his musical
    career as a(n) _____.

3. Beethoven wrote _____ symphonies, far fewer than
    either Haydn or Mozart, but all masterpieces.

4. A brass instrument Beethoven added to the symphony orches-
    tra was the _____.

5. In his ninth symphony, Beethoven made a remarkable change
    in the structure and makeup of the symphony by adding
    _____ in the last movement.

6. Beethoven's sixth symphony, which is programmatic in
    nature is known as the _____ symphony.

7. The sixth symphony is also unusual in that it has _____
    movements, rather than the traditional four.

8. Beethoven was afflicted by one of the most devastating
    handicaps that can be suffered by a musician, he was deaf.

9. Beethoven's third symphony is entitled _____,
    and was originally written as a tribute to _____.

10. In his third symphony, Beethoven replaced the traditional
    slow second movement with a _____ _____,
    and the traditional minuet third movement with a _____.

11. In his fifth symphony, sometimes called the "Fate" sym-
    phony, Beethoven used a simple four-note _____
    in the first movement, cited by Beethoven himself as
    representing "fate knocking at the door."

12. The second movement of Beethoven's fifth symphony is in
    what musical form? _____.

13. The text for the voice parts in the finale of Beethoven's
    ninth symphony is taken from the "Ode to Joy" by the
    German post _____.

14. Beethoven's compositional style is broken up into _____
    different periods.

15. Beethoven's younger contemporary, Franz Schubert, wrote
    _____ symphonies, of which the eighth, the so-called

"Unfinished" is the best-known.

<u>LISTENING STUDY GUIDE</u>

LISTEN TO EACH OF THE INDICATED MUSIC EXAMPLES
AND ANSWER THE FOLLOWING QUESTIONS:

EXAMPLE 1: BEETHOVEN: <u>SYMPHONY #5, FIRST MOVEMENT</u>
<u>SIDE 5, BAND 1</u>
1. The theme of this movement is comprised of how many notes?
    a. Three
    b. Four
2. This movement has a slow introduction.
    a. True
    b. False
3. What solo instrument is prominently featured in this movement?
    a. Oboe
    b. Flute
4. The tonality of this movement is:
    a. Major
    b. Minor
5. This movement closes with a:
    a. Recapitulation
    b. Coda

EXAMPLE 2: BEETHOVEN: <u>SYMPHONY #5, SECOND MOVEMENT</u>
<u>SIDE 5, BAND 2</u>
1. The tempo of this movement is probably:
    a. Allegro
    b. Andante
2. The form of this movement is:
    a. Sonata
    b. Theme and Variations
3. The meter of this movement is:
    a. Duple
    b. Triple
4. The second movement contrasts with the first in:
    a. Tempo and Key
    b. Orchestral texture
5. Like the first movement, this movement closes with a:
    a. Recapitulation
    b. Coda

EXAMPLE 3: BEETHOVEN: <u>SYMPHONY #5, THIRD MOVEMENT</u>
<u>SIDE 5, BAND 1</u>
1. The opening theme of this movement is:
    a. Ascending
    b. Descending

2. The tempo of this movement is probably:
   a. Allegro
   b. Adagio
3. The form of this movement is:
   a. Binary
   b. Ternary
4. The opening theme is played by:
   a. Low strings
   b. Low brasses
5. The trio section begins with which instruments?
   a. String bass and cellos
   b. Violas and violins

EXAMPLE 4: BEETHOVEN: SYMPHONY #5, FOURTH MOVEMENT
                      SIDE 5, BAND 4 (3)
1. The unique relationship between the third and fourth movements is:
   a. They are in different keys
   b. They are connected
2. The tonality of this movement is:
   a. Major
   b. Minor
3. The mood of this movement is:
   a. Meditative
   b. Triumphant
4. The form of this movement is:
   a. Sonata
   b. Theme and Variations
5. The connecting link between the 3rd and 4th movements features:
   a. Trumpets
   b. Tympani

CHAPTER 14

Concertos of Mozart and His Contemporaries

A. DEVELOPMENT OF THE CLASSICAL CONCERTO
1. Musical interplay between solo instrument and orchestra
2. Developed from the Baroque Concerto
3. Relationship between soloist and orchestra
   a. Cadenza
B. STRUCTURE OF THE CLASSICAL CONCERTO
1. Usually in three movements
   a. Fast-Slow-Fast
2. First movement
   a. Combination of sonata and ritornello forms
   b. Double exposition
3. Second movement
   a. Slow, lyrical, spacious
4. Fourth movement
   a. Combination of sonata and rondo forms
C. MOZART'S CONCERTOS
1. More than forty concertos
2. 27 for piano
3. Others for violin, horn, bassoon, flute, harp
4. The first concerto for clarinet
D. OTHER CLASSICAL COMPOSERS OF CONCERTOS
1. Haydn
   a. Violin, cello, flute, oboe, trumpet, horn
   b. Harpsichord, piano
   c. Double concertos (two instruments)
2. Beethoven
   a. Five piano concertos
   b. Violin concerto
   c. Triple concerto (piano, violin, cello)

COMPLETE THE FOLLOWING:

1. The Classical concerto is a musical interplay between solo instrument and _____.

2. The earliest of the Baroque solo concertos were for _____.

3. A solo section of a concerto, usually toward the end of a movement, during which the orchestra remains silent while the soloist plays, is known as the _____.

4. A Classical concerto is usually made up of _____ movements.

5. The first movement of a Classical concerto includes some traits of the _____ principle and some of the _____ form.

6. The first movement of a Classical concerto usually begins with two _____.

7. What is the tempo of the second movement of most Classical concertos? _____.

8. The third movement of most Classical concertos has traits of both the _____ and the _____ form.

9. Essential features of the Classical concerto involve the _____ between the movements and the structural uses of _____ and _____.

10. Mozart, a remarkable child prodigy, was said to have written a piano concerto when he was only _____ years old.

11. More than half of Mozart's concertos are for which instrument? _____.

12. Occasionally concertos were written for more than one solo instrument, as in Haydn's concerto for _____, _____ and strings.

13. Beethoven infused the concerto with even greater _____ and _____.

14. How many piano concertos did Beethoven write? _____.

15. How many violin concertos did Beethoven write: _____.

LISTEN TO EACH OF THE INDICATED MUSIC EXAMPLES
AND ANSWER THE FOLLOWING QUESTIONS

EXAMPLE L: MOZARD: <u>PIANO CONCERTO #17</u>
<u>SIDE 6, BAND 1</u>

1. The movement begins with:
    a. Orchestra alone
    b. Soloist alone
2. The meter of this movement is:
    a. Duple
    b. Triple
3. How many themes does this movement contain?
    a. Five
    b. Three
4. The cadenza follo-s which section of the movement?
    a. Development
    b. Recapitulation
5. What are the only brass instruments in this movement?
    a. Horns
    b. Trumpets

CHAPTER 15

Chamber Music of Haydn, Mozart, and Beethoven

A. THE NATURE OF CHAMBER MUSIC
    1. Music written for a small group of performers
    2. One player to a part
    3. Usually without a conductor
B. STRING ENSEMBLES
    1. String Quartet
        a. Two violins, one siola, one cello
    2. String Trio, Quintet, Sextet, etc.
        a. Various combinations of string instruments
    3. Piano Quartet or Quintet
        a. Addition of a piano to a String Trio or to a
           String Quartet
C. THE STRING QUARTET
    1. Structure is similar to that of the symphony
    2. Most important type of chamber music
    3. Major composers of String Quartets
        a. Haydn
           (1) Early quartets called divertimenti
           (2) Opus 76, #3 String Quartet called the
               "Emperor," since it includes the Austrian
               National Anthem, which Haydn himself
               wrote.
        b. Mozart
           (1) More equal emphasis to all four instru-
               ments
            (a) More demanding viola and cello parts
        c. Beethoven
           (1) Early quartets are Classical in style
           (2) Middle quartets are Romantic in style

                    (3) Late quartets are extremely complex and
                        advanced for their time
              d. Schubert
                    (1) Lyrical in style
                    (2) Best-known string work includes piano
                        (a) The "Trout" Quintet
                            (i) Piano, violin, viola, cello and
                                 string bass
                            (ii) Theme of 4th movement (of 5) is
                                 a set of variations on his song
                                 of the same name
      D. THE SONATA
          1. Sonata cycle for solo instrument
              a. Piano, or solo instrument with piano together
              b. Three or four movements, usually
          2. Major composers of sonatas
              a. Haydn wrote important piano sonatas
              b. Mozart wrote both piano and violin sonatas
              c. Schubert wrote important piano sonatas
              d. Beethoven's 32 Piano Sonatas are the epitome
                  of the genre

      COMPLETE THE FOLLOWING:

1. Chamber music is generally defined as music written for a
    _____ group of performers with _____
    player(s) to a part and without a _____.

2. The most common type of chamber music composition of the
    Classical Era was the _____ which is
    comprised of two _____, a _____
    and a _____.

3. An instrument often added to a string trio or quartet was
    the _____.

4. Classical Era chamber works usually written for one
    instrument were known as _____.

5. The string quartet usually had _____ movements, the
    forms of which were much like those in the _____.

6. A leading figure during the Classical Era in the estab-
    lishment of the string quartet as a major chamber music
    form was the composer _____.

7. Some of the above composer's early string quartets were
    called _____ by him.

8. The "Emperor Quartet" was composed by _____
    and includes as the theme of its _____ movement,

the Austrian _____ _____.

9. Mozart wrote _____ string quartets.

10. Beethoven tended to use the string quartet as a medium for
_____.

11. A prominent feature of Schubert's quartets is their
_____ quality.

12. The Classical sonata is a sonata cycle for _____,
or for _____ and another instrument.

13. Sonatas usually have _____ movements; if any movement is eliminated it would be the _____
movement.

14. The leading composer of piano sonatas during the Classical
Era was _____.

15. Other important composers of piano sonatas during the
Classical Era were _____, _____ and
_____.

LISTENING STUDY GUIDE

LISTEN TO EACH OF THE INDICATED MUSIC EXAMPLES
AND ANSWER THE FOLLOWING QUESTIONS

EXAMPLE 1: HAYDN: STRING QUARTET, OPUS 76/3
("EMPEROR")
SIDE 6, BAND 2
1. This movement begins with a slow introduction.
   a. True
   b. False
2. The tonality of this movement is:
   a. Major
   b. Minor
3. How many violins are playing?
   a. One
   b. Two
4. The meter is:
   a. Duple
   b. Triple
5. The tempo is probably:
   a. Adagio
   b. Allegro

EXAMPLE 2: BEETHOVEN: PIANO SONATA, OPUS 13
("PATHETIQUE")
SIDE 6, BAND 3

1. This movement is in which tonality?
    a. Major
    b. Minor
2. The meter of this movement is:
    a. Duple
    b. Triple
3. The tempo of this movement is probably:
    a. Allegro
    b. Andante
4. The form of this movement is:
    a. Sonata
    b. Rondo
5. In addition to the principal, recurring, theme, how many more themes are there in this movement?
    a. Two
    b. Three

CHAPTER 16

Vocal Music of the Late Eighteenth Century

A. OPERA WAS A MAJOR VOCAL FORM OF THE CLASSICAL ERA
   1. The special nature of opera
   2. The conventions of opera
      a. A sung play
      b. Plot and characters condensed and stylized
      c. Texts are short and sketchy
   3. The materials of opera
      a. Solo voices
         (1) Heroine is usually a soprano
            (a) Coloratura
            (b) Prima Donna
         (2) Other female voices include the mezzo-soprano and the contralto
         (3) Hero is usually the tenor or baritone, but rarely the bass.
         (4) "Trouser," or "Pants" roles
      b. Arias and recitatives are sung
      c. Choruses and ensembles
      d. The opera orchestra
      e. The libretto
      f. Scenery and staging
      g. Conductor and Stage Director
   4. Serious and Comic Operas
      a. Opera Seria
      b. Opera Buffa
      c. Singspiel
   5. Important Classical Era opera composers
      a. Beethoven
         (1) Only one opera, <u>Fidelio</u>, but a major work

                    b. Gluck
                        (1) Reformed opera from its Baroque excesses,
                            with his <u>Orfeo ed Eurydice</u>
                    c. Mozart
                        (1) Major opera composer of the Classical
                        (2) Italian Operas
                            (a) <u>The Marriage of Figero</u>
                            (b) <u>Don Giovanni</u>
                            (c) <u>Cosi Fan Tutte</u>
                        (3) German Operas
                            (a) <u>The Abduction from the Seraglio</u>
                            (b) <u>The Magic Flute</u>
    B. OTHER TYPES OF VOCAL MUSIC
        1. Oratorios
            a. Haydn's <u>The Creation</u> and <u>The Seasons</u>
        2. Masses
            a. Haydn's "Lord Nelson" Mass
            b. Mozart's <u>Requiem Mass</u>
            c. Beethoven's great <u>Missa Solemnis</u>

COMPLETE THE FOLLOWING:

1. The major vocal form of the late eighteenth century was
    probably _____.

2. The above vocal form is like a drama, except that the
    characters _____, rather than their lines,
    and unlike drama, the plot and characters are condensed
    and _____.

3. The operatic heroine is almost always sung by a _____
    _____.

4. If the above voice sings with a virtuosic display of high
    notes, trills, arpeggios and other ornaments, that voice
    is referred to as a _____.

5. The leading female singer in an opera is often referred
    to as the _____ _____.

6. Lower female voices appearing in operas are the _____
    _____ and the _____.

7. The highest male voice in the opera is the _____.

8. The two lower male operativ voices are the _____
    and the _____.

9. Occasionally in opera a male part is taken by a female
    singer in man's clothing, a role referred to as a
    _____ or _____ role.

10. The two most common types of recitative in opera of the Classical Era are that accompanied by continuo only, known as _____ and that accompanied by more instruments, known as _____.

11. Groups of singers in operas, such as duets, trios, quartets, etc., are usually referred to as _____.

12. The text or script of an opera is called the _____ _____, which means "little book."

13. Since many operas are in languages foreign to the audiences hearing them, opera programs usually furnish a _____ of each act.

14. Two important figures in producing an opera successfully are the conductor and the _____.

15. Major Classical Era opera composers are _____, _____, _____ and _____.

16. Comic opera is referred to as _____ in Italian, and _____ in German.

17. Non-comic opera is referred to as _____ _____, in which style Mozart wrote two works: _____ and _____.

18. Two Mozart operas notable for a fusion of both comic and serious elements are _____ and _____.

19. In the German comic opera, the dialogue is _____ rather than sung.

20. Beethoven's only opera is entitled _____.

21. The librettist for Mozart's principal Italian operas was the Italian poet _____.

22. Haydn wrote two major oratorios, entitled _____ _____ and _____.

23. Haydn's "D-Minor Mass" is generally known as the "_____ _____" mass.

24. Beethoven's only oratorio is entitled _____.

25. Beethoven's great choral/orchestral masterwork is his monumental sacred vocal work entitled the _____ _____.

LISTENING STUDY GUIDE

LISTEN TO EACH OF THE INDICATED MUSIC EXAMPLES
AND ANSWER THE FOLLOWING QUESTIONS

EXAMPLE 1: MOZART: THE MARRIAGE OF FIGARO: OVERTURE
SIDE 6, BAND 4

1. This overture is in sonata form without a:
    a. Development
    b. Recapitulation
2. The tonality of this overture is:
    a. Major
    b. Minor
3. The opening theme is presented by strings and:
    a. Oboe
    b. Bassoon
4. How many major themes are heard?
    a. Four
    b. Three
5. What is the probable tempo of this overture?
    a. Allegro
    b. Adagio

EXAMPLE 3: MOZART: THE MARRIAGE OF FIGARO: ACT I
SIDE 6, BAND 5

1. The first voice heard is that of Figaro, a:
    a. Baritone
    b. Tenor
2. The opening words are numbers (five, ten, twenty, etc.), and involve:
    a. Counting money
    b. Measuring a room
3. The second character involved in this scene is Susanna, a(n):
    a. Soprano
    b. Alto
4. The tonality of this scene is primarily:
    a. Major
    b. Minor
5. How many principal themes are used in this scene?
    a. Two
    b. Three

CHAPTER 17

Introduction to Nineteenth-Century Romanticism in Music

KEY TERMS, CONCEPTS, IMPORTANT NAMES

A. THE ROMANTIC MOVEMENT
1. A way of perceiving and dealing with the world
2. Accelerating change and ceaseless novelty
3. Individualism
4. The Artist as both a Hero and a Rebel
5. Interaction of all of the Arts
    a. Music was often inspired by painting and poetry

B. MELODY AND RHYTHM
1. Lyrical melodies
2. Rhythmic experimentation

C. HARMONY AND TEXTURE
1. Harmonic experimentation
    a. Using harmony for emotional effects
    b. Increased use of chromaticism
    c. Increased use of modulation
    d. More frequent use of dissonance
2. Greater variety and complexity of texture

D. TIMBRE AND DYNAMICS
1. Larger orchestra, added instruments
    a. Piccolo, tuba, contrabassoon, harp
    b. Additional percussion instruments
2. Enlarged choruses
3. Increased importance of Wind Bands
4. Both gradual and sudden dynamic changes, ranging from subtle to very dramatic

E. TYPES OF COMPOSITION AND FORM
1. Shorter Compositions
    a. Piano Pieces

            b. Songs (Lied and Chanson)
                (1) Song Cycles
        2. Longer Compositions
            a. Sonata Cycles
                1. Programmatic Symphonies
                2. Concertos (especially for piano and
                    violin)
            b. Symphonic Poems (tone poems)
            c. Overtures
            d. Incidental Music (often for plays)
        3. Choral Music and Opera
            a. Masses of symphonic proportions
            b. Opera a major art form of the century
        4. Form
            a. Rules of form often governed by emotion
            b. Much music with subjective titles
            c. Improvised compositions
    F. TRENDS IN 19TH CENTURY AMERICAN MUSIC
        1. Rise of orchestras and choral societies
            a. Boston Handel and Haydn Society
            b. New York Philharmonic Society
        2. Important Musicians in 19th Century America
            a. Theodore Thomas (1835-1905)
                1. Symphony orchestra conductor
            b. Stephen Foster (1826-1864)
                1. Songwriter for blackface minstrel shows
            c. Louis Moreau Gottschalk (1829-1932)
                (1) Concert pianist of international stature
            d. John Philip Sousa (1854-1932)
                (1) Prominent band director
            e. Edward MacDowell (1860-1908)
                (1) First major American composer

COMPLETE THE FOLLOWING:

1. The outstanding characteristic of romanticism is its
    stress on the _____ and on _____
    feeling.

2. Among the earliest expressions of Romanticism were the
    writings of _____, who stressed
    _____ _____ as the highest goal
    in life.

3. Important to the rise of the middle class during the
    Romantic Era was the _____ Revolution.

4. The artist of the Romantic period achieved unprecedented
    artistic and social _____, rejecting
    the limitations of _____ and substituting
    the ideals of social conscience and _____.

5. The Romantic Era created the concept of the artist as
   _____.

6. Second only to the theme of Romantic individualism was
   the theme of _____.

7. The Romantic Era was also marked by a general curiosity
   about the _____.

8. The archetypal Romantic hero was the English poet, Lord
   _____.

9. The chief exponent of Romanticism in painting was the
   French painter _____.

10. The music of the Romantic period was inspired, to an
    unprecedented degree by _____ and
    _____.

11. Composers during the Romantic Era sought to express the
    _____.

12. Melodic phrases in music of the Romantic Era are gener-
    ally _____ and more _____ than those
    of the Classical period.

13. While many Romantic melodies are simple, others are quite
    complex, filled with _____ motion,
    and _____.

14. Rhythm in Romantic music varies from the _____
    to the _____, Romantic composers often
    experimenting with new _____, and with changes
    of rhythmic _____ and _____ within a
    movement.

15. In Romantic music, tonality is often a means of achieving
    striking _____ effects.

16. Romantic harmony also makes increasing use of _____
    _____.

17. As chords were increasingly embellished with accidentals
    and modified in the course of key changes, Romantic music
    became more _____.

18. The texture of Romantic music is basically _____,
    but with an occasional touch of Baroque _____.

19. Romantic music was most often written either for very
    _____ or very _____ groups.

20. With the expansion of the orchestra during the Romantic Era, came an increase in the _____ range.

21. Short compositions such as nocturnes, etudes and impromptus were usually written for the _____.

22. Principal small vocal forms during the Romantic Era were known as _____ in Germany and as _____ in France.

23. The principal major orchestral work continued to be the _____ during the Romantic Era, but with extramusical associations to it, making it _____ _____.

24. A one-movement orchestral composition with extramusical associations, which was popular during the Romantic Era was the _____ _____.

25. The orchestral overture usually served as the introduction to a(n) _____ or a(n) _____.

26. During the Romantic Era the Mass and the oratorio became somewhat more _____, _____ and more _____.

27. The most popular large vocal form of the 19th Century was _____.

28. Romantic composers trusted more to the validity of _____ than to any rules of form.

29. The individual most responsible for the rise of the symphony orchestra in 19th-Century America was Theodore _____.

30. Important composers in 19th-Century America included the songwriter _____, the virtuoso pianist _____, the march composer _____ and the German-trained classical composer _____.

INDICATE WHICH OF THE FOLLOWING IS MORE DESCRIPTIVE OF THE CLASSICAL (C) PERIOD OR THE ROMANTIC (R) PERIOD:

1. _____ Large choirs and bands
2. _____ Melodies built on motives and short phrases
3. _____ Greater variety of meters and rhythmic patterns
4. _____ Phrases usually very regular in length.
5. _____ Symphonic poems and solo song cycles

6. _____ Clear meters
7. _____ Dense texture
8. _____ Rondo form
9. _____ Miniature forms for solo instruments
10. _____ Continued growth of orchestra

CHAPTER 18

Piano Music: Chopin and Liszt

KEY TERMS, CONCEPTS AND IMPORTANT TITLES

A. DIRECTIONS IN PIANO MUSIC
    1. The piano music of Schubert and Beethoven
        foreshadow the Romantic piano style.
        a. Piano pieces with subjective titles
        b. Piano pieces not in sonata form
    2. Early Romantic Works
        a. Robert Schumann (1810-1856)
            (1) Collections of short, "character" pieces
        b. Felix Mendelssohn (1809-1847)
            (1) Songs Without Words for piano
    3. Later noted composers of piano music
        a. Johannes Brahms (1833-1897) (German)
        b. Edvard Grieg (1843-1907) (Norwegian)
        c. Isaac Albeniz (1860-1909) (Spanish)
        d. Sergei Rachmaninov (1873-1943) (Russian)
B. CHOPIN'S PIANO MUSIC
    1. Frederick Chopin (1810-1849)
        a. Polish born, lived most of his life in France
        b. Died of tuberculosis at the age of 19
    2. Piano Style
        a. Legato (connected) style, aided by pedalling
        b. Rubato ("robbing") style of rhythmic
            displacement
        c. Very lyrical style
    3. Collections of piano music in specific forms
        a. Nocturnes (Night Pieces)
            (1) Learned from Irish pianist, John Field
                (1782-1837)
        b. Etudes (Study Pieces)
        c. Preludes (in all major and minor keys)

        d. Dances
           (1) Mazurkas (Polish dance)
           (2) Polonaises (Ceremonial Polish dance)
           (3) Waltzes
        e. Ballades
        f. Scherzos
        g. Sonatas (long, complex works)
  C. LISZT'S PIANO MUSIC
      1. Franz Liszt (1811-1886)
        a. Hungarian, lived in France, Germany, Italy
        b. Brilliant concert pianist
           (1) Transcribed symphonies and operas for
               keyboard
        c. Compositions
           (1) Sonata in B Minor
           (2) Virtuosic Etudes
           (3) <u>Anees de pelerinage</u>
              (a) Cycle of character pieces
           (4) Hungarian Rhapsodies

COMPLETE THE FOLLOWING:

1. While earlier composers for solo piano devoted themselves largely to the sonata, Romantic composers often preferred _____ pieces, with less well-defined _____ _____.

2. Romantic composers were also likely to choose _____ _____ titles and _____ associations for their piano works rather than the simple key designations used by earlier composers.

3. The composer Schumann wrote collections of short piano works, usually referred to as _____ pieces, with descriptive, even fanciful names.

4. Other important Romantic Era composers of piano music were the Germans _____ and _____, the Norwegian _____, the Spaniard _____, and the Russian _____.

5. The two major composers of piano music during the 19th Century, however, were the Polish composer _____, and the Hungarian composer _____.

6. Chopin wrote much of his piano music in a somewhat connected style, known as _____, often aided by a skillful use of the _____ pedal of the piano.

7. Chopin also used a rhythmic technique known as _____ _____, which involved small displacements inrhythm for expressive purposes.

8. Among Chopin's most celebrated works for piano are his "night" pieces, or _____, a form first conceived by the Irish pianist, John _____.

9. The above works are ardent works characterized by a long, lyrical _____ set over a _____ or _____ accompaniment.

10. A type of piano work written by Chopin which dealt with a particular aspect of piano technique being, in fact, "studies" for the piano, were known as _____.

11. Three dance types used by Chopin in his piano music were the Polish dances, the _____ and the _____, and the Austrian dance, popular throughout Europe, the _____.

12. Other forms used by Chopin in his piano compositions include the _____, the _____ and the _____.

13. One of Chopin's closest friends and confidantes was the writer Aurore Dudevant, better known by her pen name, _____ _____.

14. Chopin died of tuberculosis at the age of _____.

15. Like Chopin, Hungarian-born Franz Liszt gained early recognition in the City of _____, then settled in the City of _____.

16. Liszt became a great piano virtuoso, and was very much influenced in choosing this life style by the career of the great violin virtuoso _____.

17. Liszt treated the piano in a very _____ manner, using much of the keyboard and even playing his own transcriptions of larger works, such as Beethoven's _____ _____.

18. Like Chopin, Liszt wrote a collection of piano "study" pieces, extremely virtuosio in nature, called _____ _____.

19. Liszt also wrote a large two-volume cycle of character pieces for the piano called the _____.

20. The rhapsody, a free-form 19th-Century work relying primarily on the artist's subjective organization, was _____ Rhapsodies.

LISTENING STUDY GUIDE

LISTEN TO EACH OF THE INDICATED MUSIC EXAMPLES
AND ANSWER THE FOLLOWING QUESTIONS:

EXAMPLE 1: CHOPIN: NOCTURNE IN Eb MAJOR, OPUS 9/2
SIDE 7, BAND 1

1. The left hand accompaniment is:
   a. Contrapuntal
   b. Chordal
2. How many themes are contained in this piece?
   a. Two
   b. Three
   c. Four
3. What feature normally a part of a concerto, rather than a solo piece, is found in this nocturne?
   a. Arpeggio
   b. Cadenza
4. What is the probable tempo of this piece?
   a. Adagio
   b. Andante
5. Which theme is heard most often?
   a. First
   b. Second
   c. Third

EXAMPLE 2: LISZT: HUNGARIAN RHAPSODY #6
SIDE 7, Band 2

1. What is the meter?
   a. Duple
   b. Triple
2. How many sections comprise this piece?
   a. Two
   b. Three
   c. Four
3. This rhapsody is entirely in the major mode.
   a. True
   b. False
4. This rhapsody maintains a fast tempo throughout.
   a. True
   b. False
5. There is included in this work a section usually found only in a concerto, a
   a. Modulation
   b. Cadenza

CHAPTER 19

The Art Song: Schubert and Schumann

KEY TERMS, CONCEPTS, IMPORTANT TITLES

A. THE GROWTH OF THE ART SONG
  1. Art songs and folk songs
  2. Chanson, Lied (Lieder)
     a. Free or Modified Strophic structure
     b. French songs lighter, less introspective
  3. Development of Piano
     a. Songs accompanied by piano
  4. Wealth of German Romantic poetry
  5. Use of Symbolism
     a. Imitation of Nature
     b. Narrative and emotional expression
  6. Early Art Song composers
     a. Mozart, Haydn
     b. Beethoven wrote the first song cycle, An die ferne Geliebte
B. SCHUBERT'S LIEDER
  1. Franz Schubert (1797-1828)
     a. More than 600 songs in his short life
     b. Songs are filled with pictorial writing
     c. Early songs of note
        (1) Gretchen am Spinnrade
        (2) Erikönig
     d. Song cycles
        (1) Die Schöne Muellerin
        (2) Die Winterreise
C. SCHUMANN'S LIEDER
  1. Robert Schumann (1810-1856)
     a. A wroter about music as well as composer
        (1) Neue Zeitschrift fur Musik
     b. Married to concert pianist Clara Wieck

77

         c.   Piano and Voice are equal partners in
              Schumann's songs
         d.   Song Cycles
              (1) Dichterliebe
              (2) Frauenliebe und Leben
   D.   LATER COMPOSERS OF LIEDER
        1.   Johannes Brahms (1833-1897)
        2.   Richard Wagner (1813-1883)
        3.   Gustav Mahler (1860-1911)
        4.   Hugo Wolf (1860-1903)
        5.   Richard Strauss (1864-1949)
   E.   IMPORTANT FRENCH ART SONG COMPOSERS
        1.   Hector Berlioz (1803-1869)
        2.   Gabriel Faure (1845-1924)
        3.   Claude Debussy (1862-1918)
        4.   Maurice Ravel (1875-1937)

COMPLETE THE FOLLOWING:

1. In the 19th Century, an abundant new literature developed
    for the solo voice with piano, known in France as the
    _____, and in Germany and Austria as the
    _____.

2. The first major composer of the above vocal form in
    Austria was Franz _____.

3. Beethoven also wrote songs, and wrote the first complete
    song _____, entitled _____ _____
    _____ _____.

4. Two factors which contributed to the rise of the art song
    during the nineteenth century were the continued develop-
    ments in the ideal accompanying instrument for songs, the
    _____, and an outpouring of lyrical _____
    _____.

5. Three major poets of this era whose poetry was much-used
    by 19th Century art song composers were _____,
    _____ and _____.

6. The Lied is a partnership between poetry and _____
    as it is between piano and _____.

7. Schubert, the great 19th-Century Lied composer, wrote
    more than _____ art songs, often as many as _____
    in one day, but died tragically young at the age of _____.

8. One of Schubert's first great art songs, based on a scene
    from Goethe's _____, is entitled _____
    _____.

9. Another of Schubert's early song masterpieces, also a
    setting of a Goethe poem is his _____.

10. Although Beethoven composed the first art song cycle,
    Schubert also wrote two major song cycles, the first of
    which is entitled _____.

11. In addition to his many songs, Schubert also wrote _____
    symphonies, and much chamber music, including a well-known
    piano quintet called _____, based on one of
    his own songs.

12. The next great art song composer after Schubert was
    Robert _____.

13. The above-named composer was at first only interested in
    music for the _____, and was also active
    as a writer on music and as a music _____.

14. Schumann married _____, the daughter of
    his piano teacher, a woman who would become one of the
    leading piano virtuosos of the 19th Century.

15. Schumann wrote several major song cycles, including
    _____ and _____.

16. In addition to his songs, Schumann also wrote _____
    symphonies, and concertos for _____, _____,
    and _____, plus a great many shorter works for
    the _____.

17. A composer who was a close friend of Robert and Clara
    Schumann and who was a major composer of art songs was
    Johannes _____.

18. A composer primarily known as an opera composer, but who
    wrote one notable song cycle, the "Wesendonck Lieder,"
    was _____.

19. Leading art song composers of the late 19th and early
    20th centuries include _____, _____,
    and _____.

20. Leading composers of French art song (chansons) during
    the late 19th and early 20th centuries include _____
    _____, _____, _____ and
    _____.

LISTENING STUDY GUIDE

LISTEN TO EACH OF THE INDICATED MUSIC EXAMPLES
AND ANSWER THE FOLLOWING QUESTIONS:

Example 1: SCHUBERT: <u>DIE SCHÖNE MUELLERIN: DAS WANDERN</u>
SIDE 7, BAND 3

1. The form of this song is:
   a. Through-composed
   b. Strophic
2. The right hand of the piano accompaniment features:
   a. Chords
   b. Arpeggios
3. The voice part enters with what kind of melody?
   a. Conjunct
   b. Disjunct
4. The singer is a:
   a. Tenor
   b. Varitone
5. The texture is primarily:
   a. Polyphonic
   b. Homophonic

EXAMPLE 2: SCHUMANN: <u>WIDMUNG</u>
SIDE 7, BAND 4

1. The meter of this song is:
   a. Duple
   b. Triple
2. The form of the song is:
   a. Binary
   b. Ternary
3. The arpeggios in the piano accompaniment in the first part of the song changes to what in the second part of the song?
   a. Imitative phrases
   b. Chords
4. This song is in the major mode throughout
   a. True
   b. False
5. The texture of this song is:
   a. Homophonic
   b. Monophonic

CHAPTER 20

Symphony and Concerto: Brahms and Tchaikovsky

<u>KEY TERMS, CONCEPTS AND IMPORTANT NAMES</u>

A. THE ROMANTIC SYMPHONY
    1. The late symphoni.s of Mozart, Haydn and Schubert lead to the Romantic style
    2. Beethoven spans both the Classical and the Romantic styles with his symphonies
    3. The Program Symphony
    4. The Abstract Symphony
        a. Lyricism
        b. Rhythmic variety
        c. Harmonic characteristics
            (1) Chromaticism
            (2) Chords with added tones
            (3) Remote key relationships
        d. Increasingly denser texture
        e. Contrasts in timbre and melody
        f. Freedom from the restrictions of Classical forms
B. THE ROMANTIC CONCERTO
    1. Greater importance of melody
    2. Chromaticism
    3. Modulation to remotely related keys
    4. Soloist more important than orchestra
        a. Emphasis on virtuosity
    5. Freer interplay between soloist and orchestra
C. JOHANNES BRAHMS (1833-1897)
    1. German born
    2. Began as a violin accompanist
    3. Close friendship with the Schumanns
    4. Wrote four symphonies

                a. First symphony is often compared to
                    Beethoven's works, sometimes called
                    "Beethoven's Tenth."
    D. PETER ILYICH TCHAIKOWSKY (1840-1893)
        1. Russian born
        2. Known for his great melodic gifts
        3. Wrote six symphonies
        4. Excellent ballet composer
                a. Swan Lake, The Nutcracker
    E. LATER COMPOSERS OF ROMANTIC SYMPHONIES
        1. Cesar Franck (1822-1890)
        2. Anton Bruckner (1824-1896)
                a. Ten Symphonies
    F. IMPORTANT ROMANTIC COMPOSERS OF CONCERTOS
        1. Chopin: Two piano concertos
        2. Liszt: Three piano concertos
        3. Schumann: Concertos for piano, cello and
                violin
        4. Tchaikovsky: Concertos for piano and violin
        5. Brahms: Two piano concertos

COMPLETE THE FOLLOWING:

1. The roots of the Romantic symphony can be found in the
    late works of _____ and _____
    in a number of the symphonies written by _____
    and in the symphonic works of _____.

2. Of Schubert's symphonies, his last is probably his best,
    but his most popular symphony is his two-movement usually
    referred to as the "_____" Symphony.

3. Two 19th-Century composers who sought a new basis for
    symphonic writing were _____ and _____;
    the product of their experiments was the _____
    _____ symphony.

4. A symphony which has no extra-musical meaning, standing
    on its own as pure music, is often referred to as a(n)
    _____ symphony, a type of symphony written
    by _____ and _____ during
    the early 19th Century and by _____ and
    _____ during the late 19th Century.

5. A chord frequently used in 19th-Century harmonic writing
    was a _____ chord with an added _____.

6. Texture of the symphony of the Romantic age became
    increasingly _____, and the range of _____
    expanded greatly.

7. Contrasts in _____ as well as contrasts in
   _____ were frequently stressed.

8. Some 19th-Century symphonies had _____ movements,
   rather than the traditional _____ .

9. The final movement of Beethoven's ninth symphony expands
   symphonic structure beyond traditional concepts by adding
   _____ .

10. The composer Brahms achieved perhaps the finest synthesis
    of _____ ideal and _____ spirit in his
    symphonic works.

11. Brahms wrote _____ symphonies, and two orchestral
    overtures, the _____
    overture and the _____ overture.

12. A composer who was instrumental in furthering young
    Brahms' career by praising him in his music journal, was
    Robert _____ , with whose wife, _____ ,
    Brahms would be very close for the rest of his life.

13. Brahms was fond of the mellow sound of instruments of the
    middle register, such as the _____ ,
    _____ and _____ .

14. Brahms made notable contributions to every type of music
    except _____ .

15. In addition to his symphonies and overtures, Brahms wrote
    two concertos for _____ and one for
    _____ .

16. Like Schubert and Schumann before him, Brahms was also an
    excellent composer of _____ .

17. Tchaikovsky was educated in the Imperial Russian city
    _____ , where he was most influenced by the
    Pianist Anton _____ .

18. In addition to his symphonies, Tchaikovsky also composed
    several very popular ballets, including _____ ,
    _____ and _____ .

19. Tchaikovsky's fourth symphony was modelled on the fifth
    symphony of _____ .

20. In all, Tchaikovsky wrote _____ symphonies.

21. A Belgian composer who only wrote one symphony, but a
    work that has continued to be a popular symphony with

83

audiences, is _____.

22. An Austrian organist and church symphony who wrote ten symphonies, notable for their length and depth and for the large _____ they require was Anton _____ _____.

23. Another Austrian composer of large-scale symphonies was _____, and a Czechoslovakian composer who became an important composer of symphonies was _____.

24. In the 19th Century concerto, the _____ part was usually more prominent than the _____ part.

25. Perhaps in response to Romantic individualism, _____ elements were increasingly emphasized in the 19th Century solo concerto.

26. Chopin wrote _____ concertos for _____.

27. Schumann wrote concertos for three different instruments, the _____, the _____ and the _____.

28. Two of Tchaikovsky's important concerto works are his first concerto for _____ and his _____ concerto.

29. Although changed in many ways during the 19th Century, the solo concerto retained the traditional _____ movements.

LISTENING STUDY GUIDE

LISTEN TO EACH OF THE INDICATED MUSIC EXAMPLES
AND ANSWER THE FOLLOWING QUESTIONS:

EXAMPLE 1: BRAHMS: SYMPHONY #3: FIRST MOVEMENT
SIDE 7, BAND 5
   1. The texture of the opening bars of the symphony is:
      a. Monophonic
      b. Polyphonic
   2. This movement is entirely in the major mode
      a. True
      b. False
   3. This movement is in sonata form with what addition:
      a. Introduction
      b. Coda
   4. What percussion instruments are heard in this movement:

  a. Snare Drums
  b. Timpani
 5. How many major themes are contained in this movement?
  a. Two
  b. Three
  c. Four

EXAMPLE 2: TCHAIKOVSKY: VIOLIN CONCERTO IN D MAJOR:
           THIRD MOVEMENT
           SIDE 8, BAND 1
 1. The basic form of this movement is:
  a. Sonata
  b. Rondo
 2. The cadenza usually occurs at the close of a
  movement. Where does it occur in this movement"
  a. In the middle
  b. At the beginning
 3. How many principal themes does this movement contain?
  a. Two
  b. Three
  c. Four
 4. The meter of this movement is:
  a. Duple
  b. Triple
 5. The tempo is probably:
  a. Andante
  b. Allegro

Program Music: Mendelssohn, Berlioz, and Saint-Saëns

KEY TERMS, CONCEPTS AND IMPORTANT TITLES

A. CHARACTERISTICS OF PROGRAM MUSIC
   1. Instrumental music inspired by literary or pictorial ideas
   2. Verbal descriptions in concert programs
   3. Term "Program Music" coined by Franz Liszt
B. TYPES OF PROGRAM MUSIC
   1. Program Symphonies
   2. Symphonic Poems
   3. Concert Overtures
   4. Incidental Music
C. OVERTURES AND INCIDENTAL MUSIC
   1. Concert overtures with programmatic content
   2. Incidental music to accompany performed drama
      a. Mendelssohn: A Midsummer Night's Dream
      b. Tchaikovsky: 1812 Overture
      c. Bizet: L'Arlesienne Suite
      d. Grieg: Peer Gynt Suite
D. THE PROGRAM SYMPHONY
   1. Some contain more or fewer movements than the traditional symphony
   2. Derive some of their musical structure from nonmusical elements
   3. Idea Fixe (Berlioz)
   4. Examples:
      a. Beethoven: Pastoral Symphony
      b. Berlioz: Symphonie Fantastique
      c. Liszt: Faust Symphony
E. THE SYMPHONIC POEM (TONE POEM)
   1. A Program Symphony in one movement
   2. Evolved from the Concert Overture

3. Created by Franz Liszt
4. Examples:
   a. Liszt: _Les Preludes_
   b. St.-Saens: _Danse Macabre_
      (1) Uses scordatura technique
   c. Richard Strauss: _Don Juan_

COMPLETE THE FOLLOWING:

1. The 19th Century was a time of very close relationships between the _____.

2. Also in the 19th Century, the artist became a kind of _____ hero.

3. Liszt, Berlioz and Wagner were, in addition to being composers, also accomplished _____ and _____.

4. During the 19th Century, an increasing number of symphonies were inspired by _____, even _____ ideas.

5. The term "program music" was coined by the composer _____ to define pieces with a narrative or descriptive content.

6. One of the first programmatic symphonies was Beethoven's _____ symphony, which describes his feelings upon spending a day in the country.

7. An example of a symphony based on a literary work is the symphony entitled "Harold in Italy," by _____, which is based on a widely-read 19th Century poem by the famous Romantic Era English poet, George Gordon, better known as Lord _____.

8. An example of a piece of programmatic music that relates to the visual arts, is a set of piano pieces descriptive of a visit to an art exhibit, entitled "Pictures at an Exhibition," by the Russian composer _____.

9. A popular programmatic orchestral work written to commemorate the Russian victory over Napoleon was written by _____ and is entitled the _____ Overture.

10. Types of programmatic music written during the 19th Century include _____ symphonies, symphonic _____, concert _____ and _____ music.

11. The overture was originally a one-movement orchestral work played before the first act of an _____ or _____, but as these overtures began to achieve independent concert statusk composers began to think of them as independent works, or _____ overtures.

12. Most 19th Century overtures were based on plays, but some were written to illustrate poems or to mark special occasions, such as "Calm Sea and Prosperous Voyage," composed by _____ and the "1812 Overture," composed by _____.

13. Orchestral music written for plays during the 19th Century which was not meant as an overture for the play, but which was meant to be played during the course of the drama, or between acts, was called _____ music; such music is usually performed today as a _____ for orchestra.

14. Some composers wrote both overtures and incidental music for 19th-Century plays; an example of this is the music that Mendelssohn wrote for the Shakespeare play entitled _____.

15. Mendelssohn was the grandson of a noted _____, and the son of a wealthy _____.

16. Mendelssohn played three instruments, the _____, the _____, and the _____ as well as being an administrator, music critic and _____.

17. Mendelssohn's collection entitled "Songs Without Words" is for which instrument? _____.

18. Mendelssohn wrote _____ symphonies, an oratorio entitled _____, and a popular _____ concerto.

19. One of the great programmatic symphonies of the 19th Century is the Berlioz work entitled _____ _____, a work inspired by his complex love affair with the actress Harriet _____.

20. One of the innovative compositional techniques of Berlioz was the use of a single theme which appeared in all movements of the symphony, a concept referred to as a(n) _____ _____.

21. The orchestra required for Berlioz's first symphony was unusually _____ for the time.

22. In the Berlioz Requiem, the composer calls for sixteen _____, and four spaced _____ _____.

23. A program symphony in only one movement is known as a(n) _____ poem, or _____ poem.

24. The creator of the above form was the great virtuoso concert pianist _____, whose first work in this form is entitled _____ _____.

25. Other notable composers of symphonic poems include _____, _____, _____, _____ and _____.

26. The tuning of a stringed instrument in a way other than it is normally tuned is referred to as _____.

27. Two autobiographical tone poems of Richard Strauss are entitled _____ _____ and the _____ _____.

28. Two Strauss tone poems dealing with Spanish noblemen are Don _____ and Don _____.

29. After Strauss wrote his great tone poems during the final decades of the 19th Century, he turned to the writing of _____ during the early 20th Century.

30. In his final creative years, Strauss returned to forms which were more _____ and less complex.

LISTENING STUDY GUIDE

LISTEN TO EACH OF THE INDICATED MUSIC EXAMPLES
AND ANSWER THE FOLLOWING QUESTIONS

EXAMPLE 1: BERLIOZ: SYMPHONIE FANTASTIQUE:
FOURTH MOVEMENT
SIDE 8, BAND 2

1. Where does the idee fixe occur in this movement:
    a. At the beginning
    b. In the middle
    c. At the end
2. What is the mode of this movement?
    a. Manor
    b. Minor
3. What is the meter of this movement?
    a. Duple
    b. Triple
4. How many themes does this movement contain, exclusive of the idee fixe?

        a. Two
        b. Three
5. What percussion instrument is featured prominently
    at the close of this movement?
        a. Cymbals
        b. Snare Drum

EXAMPLE 2: ST.-SAENS: DANSE MACABRE:
                       SIDE 8, BAND 3
    1. What solo instrument is featured prominently?
            a. Clarinet
            b. Violin
    2. What is the form:
            a. Ternary
            b. Binary
    3. What melody from the Catholic Mass for the Dead is
        used in this tone poem?
            a. Requiem Aeternam
            b. Dies Irae
    4. What instrument is used to "strike" the hour of
        midnight at the close of this piece?
            a. Chimes
            b. Harp
    5. What pitched percussion instrument is used prominently
        in this work?
            a. Chimes
            b. Xylophone

CHAPTER 22

Opera and Choral Music of the Nineteenth Century

KEY TERMS, CONCEPTS, IMPORTANT COMPOSERS AND WORKS

A. OPERA
    1. Chief influences are Beethoven's <u>Fidelio</u> and Mozart's <u>Don Giovanni</u>
    2. French Opera
        a. Grand Opera
            (1) Meyerbeer" Les Huguenots
            (2) Berlioz: <u>Les Troyens</u>
        b. Comic Opera (Opera Comique)
            (1) Offenbach: <u>Orphee aux Enfers</u>
        c. Lyric Opera
            1. Bizet: <u>Carmen</u>
            2. Gounod: <u>Faust</u>
        d. Late Romantic Style French Opera
            1. St.-Saens: <u>Samson et Dalila</u>
            2. Massenet: <u>Manon</u>
    3. Italian Opera
        a. Early Romantic Italian Opera
            (1) Rossini: <u>The Barber of Seville</u>
            (2) Donizetti: <u>Lucia di Lammermoor</u>
            (3) Bellini: <u>Norma</u>
        b. Giuseppe Verdi (1813-1901)
            (1) Major 19th-Century Italian opera composer
            (2) Some nationalism in his operas
            (3) Examples:
                (a) <u>La Traviata</u>
                (b) <u>Aida</u>
                (c) <u>Otello</u>
        c. Verismo Opera
            (1) "Realism," based on events in the lives

of every day people.
        (2) Examples:
           (a) Mascagni: <u>Cavalleria Rusticana</u>
           (b) Leoncavallo: <u>I Pagliacci</u>
    d. Late Romantic Italian Opera
        1. Giacomo Puccini (1858-1924)
           (a) <u>La Boheme</u>
           (b) <u>Madama Butterfly</u>
  4. German Opera
    a. Ideological Content
    b. Carl Maria von Weber (1786-1826)
        (1) <u>Der Freischütz</u>
    c. Richard Wagner (1813-1883)
        (1) Music Dramas
        (2) Leitmotiv, Gesamtkunstwerk
        (3) Theoretical Writings
        (4) Examples:
           (a) <u>Der Ring des Nibelungen</u>
           (b) <u>Tannhäuser</u>
           (c) <u>Tristan und Isolde</u>
B. CHORAL MUSIC
  1. Choruses grew to immense proportions
  2. Short Choral Works
    a. Some accompanied by piano or small
        instrumental ensemble
  3. Large Choral Works
    a. Masses, Requiems
        (1) Berlioz: <u>Grande Messe des Morts</u>
        (2) Brahms: <u>Ein Deutsches Requiem</u>
        (3) Verdi: <u>Manzoni Requiem</u>
    b. Oratorios
        (1) Mendelssohn: <u>Elijah, St. Paul</u>
        (2) Berlioz: <u>L'Enfance du Christ</u>

COMPLETE THE FOLLOWING:

1. Two pre-Romantic operas, Mozart's _____
and Beethoven's _____ were important
precursors of the Romantic opera.

2. The three national styles of opera most prominent in the
19th Century were _____, _____
and _____.

3. During the first half of the 19th Century, the City of
_____ was the center of European opera.

4. Operas with large numbers of singers and spectacular
staging was known as _____ opera in France, its
leading composer being _____.

5. A lighter type of French opera, often with spoken dialogue, was known as _____ _____ .

6. A third type of French opera was a sort of compromise between serious, heavy opera and light opera was known as _____ opera, two of its leading composers being _____ and _____ .

7. A peak of opera composition in France was reached by the composer George _____ with his opera _____ .

8. Two important French operas of the late nineteenth century were "Samson at Dalila" by _____ and "Manon" by _____ .

9. In Italian opera of the early nineteenth century, _____ _____ was strongly dominant over _____ .

10. An important composer of light Italian opera in the early years of the 19th Century was _____ , whose best-known comic opera was _____ .

11. The two most important figures in Italian opera between Rossini and Verdi were _____ and _____ .

12. Verdi, the leading composer of Italian opera during the 19th Century, first came into prominence with his biblical opera entitled _____ , which symbolized to many Italians their aspirations for independence from Austria.

13. The three major operas of the second major phase of Verdi's operatic career were _____ , _____ and _____ .

14. Verdi had a brief association with Parisian opera with his two operas entitled _____ and _____ .

15. An opera Verdi wrote for the festivities celebrating the opening of the Suez Canal was _____ , which was written in a style which combined the best aspects of both _____ grand opera and _____ opera.

16. Very late in his life, Verdi produced two operas based on Shakespeare, the tragedy _____ and the comedy _____ .

17. A late 19th-Century Italian opera style which used subject matter based on the lives of everyday people was known as _____ .

18. Two leading composers of the above operatic style were
    _____ and _____, whose
    principal operas, one-act works usually performed on the
    same evening, were _____ and
    _____.

19. One of the most popular composers of Italian opera of the
    late 19th and early 20th century was _____.

20. Two of the above composer's operas which are set in the
    Far East are _____ and _____.

21. The opera "Tosca" is set in the City of _____, and
    the opera "La Boheme" is set in the City of _____.

22. The first important composer of German Romantic opera was
    _____, his major work being entitled _____
    _____.

23. The great master of German opera of the 19th Century was
    _____, who preferred to call his operas
    _____.

24. The turning point in Wagner's evolution, and his first
    truly German opera, was _____.

25. Two Wagner operas which have religious/philosophical sub-
    jects were _____ and _____.

26. Three of Wagner's theoretical writings about opera and
    music in general are _____,
    _____, and _____.

27. Wagner proposed that all artistic aspects of a dramatic
    work be united to form a unified work of art, which he
    called a _____.

28. In his music dramas, Wagner gave each important person,
    thing or idea its own musical motive, which he referred
    to as a(n) _____.

29. Wagner's great masterwork is his monumental cycle of four
    music dramas entitled _____,
    the four parts of which are entitled _____,
    _____, _____, and
    _____.

30. Wagner's great "love" opera is entitled _____.

31. Wagner's only comedy in opera is entitled _____.

32. The chorus in the 19th Century, like the orchestra, grew

to _____ proportions.

33. Two important Requiem Masses of the 19th Century were written by _____ and _____.

34. A non-Catholic, non-Latin Requiem was written by the German composer _____.

35. Three importang oratorios of the 19th Century were Mendelssohn's two works entitled _____ and _____ and the Berlioz work entitled _____.

INDICATE WHETHER EACH OF THE FOLLOWING OPERAS IS:

GRAND OPERA   (G)
COMIC OPERA   (C)
LYRIC OPERA   (L)
MUSIC DRAMA   (M)

1. _____ Das Rheingold
2. _____ The Barber of Seville
3. _____ Parsifal
4. _____ Orpheus in the Underworld
5. _____ Mignon
6. _____ Twilight of the Gods
7. _____ The Huguenots
8. _____ Aida
9. _____ Falstaff
10. _____ The Flying Dutchman

WHO COMPOSED EACH OF THE FOLLOWING 19TH CENTURY OPERAS?

1. La Traviata _____
2. La Boheme _____
3. Lohengrin _____
4. The Barber of Seville _____
5. Fidelio _____
6. Norma _____
7. Rigoletto _____
8. Aida _____
9. Der Freischütz _____
10. Tristan und Isolde _____
11. Carmen _____
12. William Tell _____
13. Samson et Dalila _____
14. Falstaff _____
15. Lucia di Lammermore _____

LISTENING STUDY GUIDE

LISTEN TO EACH OF THE INDICATED MUSIC EXAMPLES
AND ANSWER THE FOLLOWING QUESTIONS

EXAMPLE 1: VERDI: <u>LA TRAVIATA: AH FORSE LUI & SEMPRE LIBRE</u>
SIDE 8, BAND 4

1. What is the voice classification of the singer?
    a. Soprano
    b. Mezzo
2. In which mode does the aria begin?
    a. Major
    b. Minor
3. The language is:
    a. Italian
    b. French
4. The form of the aria is:
    a. Binary
    b. Ternary
5. Each part of the aria is preceded by a(n):
    a. Arioso
    b. Recitative

EXAMPLE 2: WAGNER: <u>DIE WALKÜRE: DER RITT DER WALKÜREN</u>
SIDE 9, BAND 1

1. The Valkyrie Leitmotiv is played by the:
    a. Strings
    b. Brasses
2. The tonality of the music moves from:
    a. Minor to major
    b. Major to minor
3. The Valkyrie who sings the opening motive is a:
    a. Soprano
    b. Mezzo
    c. Contralto
4. The opening vocal line represents a:
    a. Calling motive
    b. Threatening motive
5. There are two prominent motives, one vocal and one:
    a. Choral
    b. Instrumental

EXAMPLE 3: WAGNER: <u>TRISTAN UND ISOLDE: PRELUDE</u>
SIDE 9, BAND 2

1. The melodic structure is highly:
    a. Diatonic
    b. Chromatic
2. The tempo is:
    a. Slow
    b. Fast
3. The motives are frequently:

96

        a.   Changed
        b.   Repeated
4.   The form is:
        a.   Free
        b.   Highly structured
5.   The motives are primarily:
        a.   Conjunct
        b.   Disjunct

CHAPTER 23

Nationalism and Late Romanticism

KEY TERMS, CONCEPTS, IMPORTANT NAMES AND TITLES

A. NATIONALISM IN MUSIC
    1. Focus on sounds characteristic of a nation's or
        region's folk music
        a. Rolk melodies, dances and rhythms
        b. Novel harmonic systems
    2. National opera plots
    3. Nationalistic program music
    4. Use of national instruments
B. RUSSIAN NATIONALISM
    1. Glinka: A Life for the Czar
    2. "The Russian Five"
        a. Balakirev, Cui, Borodin, Mussorgsky,
            Rimsky-Korsakov
        b. Example:
            (1) Mussorgsky: Pictures at an Exhibition
C. BOHEMIAN NATIONALISM
    1. Primarily Czechoslovakian today
    2. Examples
        a. Smetana: The Bartered Bride, Ma Vlast
        b. Dvorak: Slavonic Dances
D. SPANISH NATIONALISM
    1. Albeniz: Iberia
    2. Falla: Nights in the Gardens of Spain
E. ENGLISH NATIONALISM
    1. Vaughan Williams: Fantasia on Greensleeves
    2. Holst: A Somerset Rhapsody
F. SCANDINAVIAN NATIONALISM
    1. Norway
        a. Grieg: Peer Gynt Suite (2)

       2. Finland
         a. Sibelius: Finlandia
  G. LATE ROMANTICISM
       1. Germany and Austria
         a. The Romantic impulse became intensified and
           exaggerated
         b. Increased orchestral size, denser texture
         c. Gustav Mahler (1860-1911)
           (1) Symphony #8: "Symphony of a Thousand"
           (2) Lieder eines fahrenden Gesellen
         d. Richard Strauss (1864-1949)
           (1) Salome
         e. Arnold Schoenberg (1874-1951)
           (1) Early works are Romantic in style
       2. France
         a. Faure: Requiem Mass
       3. Russia
         a. Rachmaninov and Scriabin
       4. Late Romanticists from other countries
         a. Sibelius (Finland), MacDowell (United
           States)

COMPLETE THE FOLLOWING:

1. Music written by 19th-Century composers to directly reflect their homelands in a variety of ways is referred to as _____ music.

2. Throughout the 17th Century _____ and _____ were regarded as the primary sources for new music, and in the 18th Century, _____ and _____ moved into prominence.

3. The melodies of nationalistic music were commonly inspired by _____ _____.

4. The rhythms of nationalistic music were often derived from _____ rhythms.

5. Nationalism was often found in 19th-Century plots and in _____ music.

6. National instruments began to appear in 19th-Century music, such as the _____ in Spanish music.

7. One of the earliest countries to become involved with nationalistic music was _____, with the composer _____, whose two operas _____ and _____ are extremely nationalistic in character.

8. A group of nationalistic composers in Russia known as "The Russian Five" included _____ - _____, _____, _____ and _____.

9. Perhaps the most nationalistic composer of the above members of "The Russian Five" was _____, whose opera _____ _____ is extremely nationalistic.

10. "Pictures at an Exhibition" was originally written for _____, but was later orchestrated by _____.

11. An area of Eastern Europe which is today a part of Czechoslovakia, which produced some important nationalistic music was the country known as _____.

12. An important Czechoslovakian nationalist composer was _____, whose opera _____ is one of his major nationalistic works.

13. Another well-known Czechoslovakian nationalist composer was _____, whose _____ Dances are important nationalistic works, and who spent some time in the United States, where he wrote his 9th symphony, which is subtitled _____.

14. The first important Spanish nationalist composer was _____, whose piano collection entitled _____ evoke the rhythms of Spanish dances.

15. Another important Spanish nationalist composer was _____, whose "Nights in the Gardens of Spain" for _____ and orchestra, and opera _____ are nationalistic in character.

16. The first English nationalist composer of note was _____, whose _____, often played at high school and college commencement exercises as a processional is an important work.

17. The major English nationalist composer was the 20th-Century composer Ralph _____ _____, who was extremely active in researching and collecting English folk music.

18. Another English composer who fostered the use of folk materials in his music was Gustav _____.

19. The leading Norwegian nationalist composer of the 19th Century was _____, whose principal nationalistic compositions are his two _____ _____ Suites.

20. The major Finnish nationalist composer of the 19th Century was _____, whose major nationalistic work, which takes the name of the country itself, is entitled

    _____.

21. Four important late Romantic composers of Germany and Austria were _____, _____, _____ and _____.

22. Mahler is best known for his _____, one of which, his eighth, calls for such an extremely large component of instruments and voices that it has been dubbed "The Symphony of a _____."

23. Mahler was also an important opera conductor and a composer of songs, including the song cycle entitled

    _____ _____.

24. The late Romantic composer Richard Strauss is known for his _____ poems, as well as for his operas, among which is the powerful one-act opera _____.

25. Two leading late Romantic composers from other countries were the French composer _____ and the great Russian pianist _____.

WHICH COUNTRY DOES EACH OF THE FOLLOWING NATIONALISTS REPRESENT?

1. De Falla _____
2. Vaughan Williams _____
3. Grieg _____
4. Glinka _____
5. Sibelius _____
6. Dvorak _____
7. Mussorgsky _____
8. Elgar _____
9. Albeniz _____
10. Smetana _____

LISTENING STUDY GUIDE

LISTEN TO EACH OF THE INDICATED MUSIC EXAMPLES AND ANSWER THE FOLLOWING QUESTIONS

EXAMPLE 1: MUSSORGSKY: PICTURES AT AN EXHIBITION:
                        PROMENANDE AND GNOMUS:
                        SIDE 9, BAND 3

1. The opening theme of Promenade is played by a:
   a. Clarinet
   b. Trumpet
2. This theme is then harmonized by the:
   a. Strings
   b. Brasses
3. Gnomus is in which mode?
   a. Major
   b. Minor
4. How many themes are presented in Gnomus?
   a. Two
   b. Three
   c. Four
5. This music was originally written for:
   a. Piano
   b. Orchestra
   c. Chamber Ensemble

EXAMPLE 2: MAHLER: LIEDER EINES FAHRENDEN GESELLEN:
                     GING HEUT' MORGEN ÜBER'S FELT
                     SIDE 9, BAND 4

1. The song opens happily and closes:
   a. Happily
   b. Sadly
2. The form is:
   a. Modified Strophic
   b. Through-Composed
3. The meter is:
   a. Duple
   b. Triple
4. The singer is a:
   a. Tenor
   b. Baritone
5. The tempo is probably:
   a. Andante
   b. Allegro

CHAPTER 24

Introduction to Early Twentieth-Century Music

KEY TERMS, CONCEPTS, IMPORTANT COMPOSERS AND WORKS

A. BACKGROUND
1. Material progress
2. World Wars
3. Artistic Movements: Cubism, Surrealism
4. Literary Movements: Experimental writing
   a. Stream-of-consciousness
5. Modern Dance
B. TRENDS IN EARLY TWENTIETH CENTURY MUSIC
1. Impressionism
   a. Claude Debussy (1862-1918)
2. Objectivity
3. Primitivism
4. Nationalism
5. Futurism
   a. Microtonal composition
6. Gebrauchamusik
   a. Paul Hindemith (1895-1963)
7. Light, satirical music
8. Music of a machine culture
9. Jazz
10. Neoclassicism
11. Expressionism
    a. Atonality
    b. Serialism
12. Electronic music
C. MELODY AND RHYTHM
1. Melodic variety
   a. Less lyricist, fewer embellishments
   b. Motives and phrases of irregular length
   c. Some music with no tonal center

        2. Rhythmic innovations
            a. Ostinato
            b. Rhythmic vagueness
            c. Frequent changes in meter
    D. HARMONY AND TEXTURE
        1. New harmonic techniques
            a. Pandiatonicism
            b. Bitonality
            c. Polytonality
            d. Renewed interest in counterpoint
    E. TIMBRE
        1. Stress on percussive sounds
        2. Use of electronic instruments
    F. TYPES OF COMPOSITION AND FORM
        1. Innovative compositions expanding the
            definition of certain genres
        2. Greatly altered traditional forms
    G. TRENDS IN 20TH CENTURY AMERICAN MUSIC
        1. French Influence
            a. Impressionism
                (1) Charles Griffes (1884-1920)
            b. Nadia Boulanger (1887-1979)
        2. Nationalism
            a. George Gershwin (1898-1937)
                (1) Rhapsody in Blue
                (2) Porgy and Bess
        3. Traditionalism
            a. Neoromantics
                (1) Samuel Barber (1910-1981)
                    (a) Adagio for Strings
            b. Neoclassicists
                (1) Walter Piston (1894-1976)
                    (a) The Incredible Flutist
        4. Progressivism
            a. Roger Sessions (1896-1985)
                (1) The Black Maskers
        5. Experimentalism
            a. Charles Ives (1874-1954)
            b. Henry Cowell (1897-1965)
                (1) Experiments with piano: tone clusters,
                    playing inside the piano
                (2) The Banshee

COMPLETE THE FOLLOWING:

1. A new style of art appearing in the early 20th Century was
    known as _____, its first proponent being the
    painter Pablo _____.

2. Another new style of 20th-Century art was known as

surrealism, a few of its leading painters being _____ _____, _____ and _____.

3. A 20th-Century literary style known as stream-of-consciousness was founded by James _____ in his novel _____.

4. Classical ballet evolved into modern dance during the 20th Century, following the leads of the entrepreneur _____ _____, and the dancer/choreographer Martha _____.

5. A major musical movement of the late 19th and early 20th centuries was _____, established by the French composer _____.

6. An important trend among composers in the years after World War I was an emphasis on _____.

7. Another artistic trend following World War I was an interest in _____ art as a source of inspiration.

8. An early 20th Century movement in the arts which looked for a revolutionary new aesthetic to make it compatible with the modern world was known as _____.

9. A musical style that was intended to be easily understood by the general public was known as _____, its leading proponent being the composer _____.

10. A major musical style born not in Europe but in the United States, which came into world-wide prominence during the 1920s was _____.

11. Some composers, in order to counter the excesses of the Romantic era, espoused a return to more traditional styles of composing in a movement known as _____.

12. A new kind of 20th-Century music which was constructed in such a way as to avoid any central tonality or key center came to be known as _____.

13. A 20th Century musical system which used all twelve notes of the chromatic scale equally, setting them down in a structured "tone row" was known as _____.

14. Both of the musical styles of #12 and #13 above are usually referred to as _____.

15. An early move toward the use of tape-recorders and other electronic devices in creating music began in France in

the 1940s in a style known as _____,
which developed into a broader style known as _____
music.

16. Melody in 20th-Century music was often built upon motives
    of irregular _____, or restricted to small
    movements within a narrow _____, or even com-
    pletely lacking any _____ center.

17. In addition to the traditional major, minor and chromatic
    scales, 20th-Century music often used _____ and
    _____ scales, as well as the Mediaeval Church
    _____.

18. Twentheth-century rhythm was varied and complex, often
    unified by a stubbornly repeated rhythmic pattern called
    a(n) _____.

19. A factor contributing to the dynamic energy of much 20th-
    Century music involved frequent changes in _____.

20. The harmonic practice of superimposing two different
    tonalities was known as _____; if more
    than two tonalities were superimposed, the technique was
    known as _____.

21. Single notes or short motives presented in rapidly con-
    trasting registers created a musical texture known as
    _____.

22. The harmonic superimposition of both the major and minor
    modes was known as _____.

23. The increased interest in rhythm among 20th-Century com-
    posers led to an increased stress on _____
    sounds.

24. A major influence on the arts following World War I was
    _____.

25. The influence of the country in #24 above was particularly
    strong on the work of the young American composer _____
    _____.

26. One of the major teachers of the 1920s was the French-
    woman Nadia _____.

27. Nationalism in 20th Century America was expressed through
    the use of jazz elements, particularly in the work of the
    young American composer _____,
    whose principal work in this style is _____.

28. Two American composers who remained traditionalists, building on the styles of the Classical and Romantic periods of music were _____ and _____.

29. Moving beyond the traditionalists into new and more progressive musical styles were composers such as the American composer _____.

30. Two important experimentalist composers of 20th-Century America were Charles _____ and Henry _____.

INDICATE WHICH OF THE FOLLOWING ARE BETTER DESCRIPTIVE OF THE MUSIC OF THE ROMANTIC ERA (R) AND WHICH ARE BETTER DESCRIPTIVE OF THE MUSIC OF THE EARLY TWENTIETH CENTURY (T):

1. _____ Long, lyrical phrases
2. _____ Atonal styles
3. _____ Importance of solo piano
4. _____ Importance of percussion instruments
5. _____ Frequently changing meters
6. _____ Wide range of textures
7. _____ Newly developed symphonic poem
8. _____ Experimentation with new harmonic methods
9. _____ Large orchestras and choirs
10. _____ Increased popularity of bands

CHAPTER 25

French Music at the Turn of the Century

KEY TERMS, CONCEPTS, IMPORTANT COMPOSERS, WORKS

A. IMPRESSIONISM
   1. Influenced by related arts
      a. Impressionist painting
      b. Symbolist poetry
   2. Claude Debussy (1862-1918)
      a. Most prominent Impressionistic composer
      b. Influenced by nature
      c. Style
         (1) Harmonic Innovations
            (a) Chord streams
            (b) Increased dissonance
            (c) Use of whole-tone scale
         (2) Changes in timbre
            (a) Veiled orchestral sound, featuring individual timbres of instruments
            (b) Use of lower and higher registers of various instruments
            (c) Frequent solos for harp, flute, oboe, English horn
         (3) Freer forms
            (a) Form emerges from subject matter of the work
         (4) Important Impressionistic works
            (a) <u>Prelude a l'apres-midi d'un faune</u>
            (b) <u>Pelleas et Melisande</u>
            (c) <u>Feux d'artifice</u>
B. LES SIX, SATIE AND RAVEL
   1. Les Six
      a. Six young French composers who espoused Neoclassicism and opposed Impressionism

        b. Arthur Honegger (1892-1955)
            (1) Oratorios: <u>King David</u> and <u>Joan of Arc</u>
                <u>at the Stake</u>
        c. Darius Milhaud (1892-1974)
            (1) <u>The Ox on the Roof</u>
        d. Francis Poulenc (1899-1963)
            (1) <u>Gloria</u>
            (2) <u>The Dialogue of the Carmelites</u>
    2. Erik Satie (1866-1925)
        a. Not a member of Les Six, but a major 20th-
            Century Neoclassicist
        b. Satire and whimsey
            (1) <u>Three pieces in the Shape of a Pear</u>
    3. Maurice Ravel
        a. Both an Impressionist and a Neoclassicist
        b. Brilliant orchestrator
        c. Examples:
            (1) <u>Concerto in G</u>
            (2) <u>Bolero</u>

COMPLETE THE FOLLOWING:

1. The term "Impressionism" was first applied to which of the
    fine arts? _____ .

2. The literary counterpart of Impressionism was the _____
    _____ movement in French poetry.

3. The first, and major, Impressionist in music is the French
    composer, Claude _____ .

4. One of the great influences on the music of the above com-
    poser was his great love of _____ .

5. A new harmonic technique in Impressionism was to repeat
    chords up and down the staff in parallel motion, a tech-
    nique known as _____ _____ .

6. The traditional chord build on thirds was expanded in
    Impressionistic music to include intervals beyond the
    scope of the octave, such as _____ , _____
    and even _____ .

7. A scale which was frequently used by Impressionist com-
    posers was the _____ scale.

8. The timbre, or tone quality, of Impressionistic music is
    unique, featuring such sounds as the lower register notes
    of the _____ and _____ , the clear high
    notes of the _____ and the muted voices of the
    _____ and _____ .

9. One of Debussy's first orchestral works in the Impressionistic style is his _____
    _____.

10. Other important Debussy Impressionistic works include his orchestral work _____ and his only opera, entitled _____.

11. Debussy wrote a great deal of piano music, including a book of 24 _____, including the brilliant composition entitled _____.

12. A group of young French composers banded together to advocate a return to clarity and simplicity in music and came to be known as "_____ _____," of whom three would become well-known, _____, _____ and _____.

13. The mentor of the above group was the satirical and whimsical Erik _____.

14. The best known of all 20th-Century French composers after Debussy was the composer and pianist Maurice _____.

15. The composer in #14 was a particularly brilliant orchestrator, a skill clearly exhibited in his ballet entitled _____.

WHO WROTE EACH OF THE FOLLOWING FRENCH COMPOSITIONS?

1. Concerto for the Left Hand
    _____

2. Prelude to "The Afternoon of a Faun"
    _____

3. The Ox on the Roof
    _____

4. Fireworks
    _____

5. King David
    _____

6. Christopher Columbus
    _____

7. The Dialogue of the Carmelites
    _____

8. Joan of Arc at the Stake
    _____

110

9.   The Blessed Demoiselle

_____

10.   La Mer

_____

LISTENING STUDY GUIDE

EXAMPLE 1: DEBUSSY: PRELUDE "A L'APRES-MIDI D'UN FAUN"
                              SIDE 9, BAND 5
1.   The opening theme is presented by a:
     a.   Clarinet
     b.   Flute
2.   A prominent string instrument heard in this work is
     the:
     a.   Cello
     b.   Harp
3.   The harmony is extremely:
     a.   Dissonant
     b.   Chromatic
4.   A unique percussion instrument used in this piece is
     (are):
     a.   Xylophone
     b.   Antique Cymbals
5.   The form of this piece is:
     a.   Binary
     b.   Ternary

EXAMPLE 2: DEBUSSY: PRELUDE: "FEUX D'ARTIFICES":
                              SIDE 9, BAND 6
1.   The rhythm of the opening section features:
     a.   Triplets
     b.   Syncopation
2.   The opening section closes with a(n):
     a.   Arpeggio
     b.   Glissando
3.   Motives from which other piece of music are quoted
     in this work?
     a.   A popular French folk song
     b.   The French National Anthem
4.   The dynamics of this work feature a long:
     a.   Crescendo
     b.   Decrescendo
5.   The meter and tempo of this piece are:
     a.   Consistent throughout
     b.   Changing throughout

111

CHAPTER 26

New Styles of Tonality

KEY TERMS, CONCEPTS, IMPORTANT NAMES AND TITLES

A. EXPERIMENTS WITH TONALITY
   1. Radically new ways of using tonality
   2. Avoidance of tonality entirely
B. TONAL COMPOSERS
   1. Bela Bartok (1881-1945)
      a. Began as Hungarian nationalist composer
      b. Influence of Liszt and Richard Strauss
      c. Melody, Rhythm
         1. Simple melodies
         2. Use of pentatonic, whole-tone and folk
            music scales
         3. Octave displacement
         4. Tone clusters
         5. Polyrhythms
      d. Texture, Timbre
         1. Contrapuntal texture
         2. Wide range of tone colors
         3. Emphasis on percussion instruments
      e. Form
         1. Motivic development using small motives
            or phrases
         2. Organic growth
      f. Examples:
         1. <u>Music for Strings, Percussion, and</u>
            <u>Celesta</u>
         2. <u>Concerto for Orchestra</u>
   1. Igor Stravinsky (1882-1971)
      a. Early works have folk music influence
      b. First major works were ballets
      c. Rhythmic innovations

           (1) Ostinato rhythms, polyrhythms
           (2) Frequent changes of meter
      d. Wide range of textures
      e. Neoclassicism
      f. Abstract principles of structure
      g. Examples:
           (1) The Rite of Spring
           (2) Symphony of Psalms
  3. Paul Hindemith (1895-1963)
      a. Gebrauchsmusik
      b. Opposed extreme harmonic innovation
           (1) Preferred to use the twelve tones of the
               chromatic scale around a tonal center
           (2) Harmony textbook: The Carft of Musical
               Composition
      c. Works
           (1) Mathis der Maler
  4. Charles Ives (1874-1954)
      a. Melody:
           (1) Quoted hymns, popular songs, folk songs,
               classics, often greatly altered
      b. Rhythm:
           (1) Use of irregular meters
           (2) Metrical inconsistency
      c. Harmony:
           (1) Disregard for chord structure and function
           (2) Polytonality, atonality
           (3) Free, dissonant counterpoint
           (4) Tone clusters
      d. Stereophonic effects
      e. Examples:
           (1) A Symphony: Holidays
           (2) Concord Sonata
  5. Aaron Copland (1900-   )
      a. Early works feature jazz rhythms, bold
         dissonances, Jewish melodies
      b. Several ballets on American themes
      c. Melody:
           (1) Conjunct, occasional larger intervals
           (2) Folk music and religious tunes
      d. Rhythm:
           (1) Rhythmic vitality, drive
           (2) Percussive rhythms, ostinato
           (3) Syncopation, changing meters
      e. Harmony:
           (1) Tonal, some polytonality
      f. Example:
           (1) Rodeo
  6. Other 20th-Century Tonal Composers
      a. Benjamin Britten (1913-1976)
           (1) Peter Grimes, Simple Symphony

b. Dimitri Shostakovish (1906-1975)
    (1) Symphonist
c. Sergei Prokoviev (1891-1953)
    (1) <u>The Classical Symphony</u>

COMPLETE THE FOLLOWING:

1. Among the most important twentieth-century composers of
    tonal music were _____, _____,
    and _____.

2. Two major twentieth-century American composers who both
    took an experimental outlook combined with a basic orien-
    tation towards tonality were _____ and _____.

3. One of the composer Bartok's chief interests in music was
    _____ and _____ music, which he used in
    his early compositions.

4. Bartok's style of harmony and his orchestration were both
    influenced by the works of _____ and
    _____, and his driving percussive rhythms
    show the influence of his great contemporary _____.

5. Bartok's melodies tend to be fairly _____,
    using, in addition to traditional scales, _____
    _____, _____ and various European
    _____ scales.

6. One interesting melodic practice that Bartok often used
    was the placing of successive notes of a melody in differ-
    ent octaves, a technique known as _____
    _____.

7. Rhythmically, Bartok occasionally made use of a type of
    rhythmic counterpoint in which several different rhythms
    proceed simultaneously, a technique known as _____.

8. Bartok made much use of _____, which were
    dissonant chords made up of several adjacent tones.

9. The form of much of Bartok's music depends greatly on his
    method of _____ development.

10. In addition to being a well-known noted composer, Bartok
    was also a noted _____ and _____.

11. Stravinsky's early use of Russian and Oriental melodies
    is due to the influence of his teacher, _____-
    _____.

12. Stravinsky's earliest compositional success were in the area of _____ .

13. Stravinsky's melodies are often motivic, but with each motive treated as part of a process of constant _____ _____ .

14. Rhythmically, Stravinsky often made use of driving _____ _____ rhythms, frequent changes of _____ and _____ .

15. Like many modern composers, Stravinsky made meticulous use of directions to performers in his scores, especially in the area of _____ and _____ markings.

16. A style Stravinsky turned to in the years following World War I was _____ , especially in his ballet entitled _____ , and his opera/oratorio _____ _____ .

17. In the years following World War I, the composer Hindemith experimented with a kind of music that was readily accessible to both performer and listener, a concept identified as _____ or "music for use."

18. An important 20th-Century music theorist, Hindemith wrote a theory textbook in the 1930s entitled "The Craft of _____ _____ ."

19. In addition to triadic harmonies (chords built on thirds), Hindemith also made use of _____ harmonies (chords built on fourths).

20. If Stravinsky represents the eclectic, radical side of tonal composition during the early 20th Century, Hindemith represents its _____ side.

21. A primary element in the music of the 20th-Century American composer Charles Ives is innovation in the use of _____ .

22. Ives was a composer only by avocation, being by profession a major figure in the _____ business.

23. Ives was so far ahead of his time that most of the conductors and performers to whom he showed his music considered it to be _____ .

24. For his melodies, Ives often drew from American _____ , popular _____ and folk _____ , as well

from well-known _____.

25. By using several different performing groups in a single composition, Ives became one of the first composers to use what would become known as _____ effects.

26. In addition to many other types of music, Ives wrote _____ symphonies and more than _____ songs.

27. The American composer Aaron Copland studied in France with the remarkable composition teacher, Nadia _____.

28. Copland's early works use _____ rhythms, bold _____ and occasional _____ melodies.

29. Copland created long melodic lines by using repeated _____ and adding new _____.

30. Copland's works, like many 20th-Century composers, have an unmistakable _____ drive.

31. Harmonically, Copland remained rather consistently _____ _____.

32. One of Copland's chief interests in composing is in the area of _____, especially with American themes.

33. One of the major tonal composers in 20th-Century England after Vaughan Williams and Elgar was Benjamin _____ _____.

34. Soviet Russia was very much opposed to new styles of composition being used by 20th-Century composers, a concept the Soviet censors referred to as _____.

35. Two Soviet composers who generally adhered to the restrictions placed on them by the Soviet censors were _____ _____ and _____.

INDICATE WHO WROTE EACH OF THE FOLLOWING COMPOSITIONS:

1. The Classical Symphony
   _____

2. Music for Strings, Percussion and Celesta
   _____

3. Mathis der Maler
   _____

4. The Rite of Spring
   _____

5. Peter Grimes

    _____

6. Appalachian Spring

    _____

7. The Unanswered Question

    _____

8. Pulcinella

    _____

9. A Symphony: Holidays

    _____

10. Rodeo

    _____

LISTENING STUDY GUIDE

EXAMPLE 1: BARTOK: MUSIC FOR STRINGS, PERCUSSION AND CELESTA
                                SIDE 10, BAND 1
   1. The melodic material is frequently:
       a. Conjunct
       b. Disjunct
   2. The principal motive has how many notes?
       a. Two
       b. Three
   3. What is the form of this movement?
       a. Rondo
       b. Sonata
   4. The same meter is used throughout the movement.
       a. True
       b. False
   5. The tempo is probably:
       a. Allegro
       b. Andante

EXAMPLE 2: STRAVINSKY: LE SACRE DU PRINTEMPS:
                           "DANSE SACRALE"
                           SIDE 10, BAND 2
   1. The metric structure of this section is:
       a. Consistent throughout
       b. Constantly changing
   2. The melodic material consists of:
       a. Long, elaborate lines
       b. Short, repeated motives
   3. The form of this section of the ballet is essentially:
       a. Sonata
       b. Rondo
   4. The harmonic structure is frequently:
       a. Homophonic
       b. Dissonant

5. The tempo is probably:
   a. Allegro
   b. Moderato

EXAMPLE 3: HINDEMITH: MATHIS DER MALER SYMPHONY:
                        SIDE 10, BAND 4
   1. The theme of the introduction is based on a German:
      a. Folk Song
      b. Chorale
   2. This movement is in what form?
      a. Sonata
      b. Theme and Variations
   3. How many themes are contained in the movement,
      exclusive of the theme of the introduction?
      a. Two
      b. Three
      c. Four
   4. Except for the introduction, the meter of this
      movement is:
      a. Duple
      b. Triple
   5. In the development section, the theme of the
      introduction is played on which instruments?
      a. Cellos
      b. Trombones

EXAMPLE 4: IVES: A SYMPHONY: HOLIDAYS: "FOURTH OF JULY"
                        SIDE 10, BAND 3
   1. The opening theme of this movement is based on an
      American:
      a. Folk Song
      b. Patriotic Song
   2. At one point, brasses play an excerpt from the
      military bugle call known as:
      a. Taps
      b. Reveille
   3. The tempo of this movement moves from:
      a. Slow to fast
      b. Fast to slow
   4. The harmony of this movement is occasionally?
      a. Atonal
      b. Bitonal
   5. An instrument featured in this movement which is not
      normally considered to be a part of the symphony
      orchestra is the:
      a. Xylophone
      b. Piano

EXAMPLE 5: COPLAND: RODEO: "HOEDOWN":
                        SIDE 10, BAND 5
   1. This movement represents a typical American:

118

       a.   Square Dance
       b.   Patriotic March
2.   The tempo of this movement is probably:
       a.   Allegro
       b.   Andante
3.   The meter is:
       a.   Duple
       b.   Triple
4.   The mode of this movement is:
       a.   Major
       b.   Minor
5.   A pitched percussion instrument featured in this
     movement is the:
       a.   Celesta
       b.   Xylophone

CHAPTER 27

Atonality and Serialism

<u>KEY TERMS, CONCEPTS, IMPORTANR NAMES AND TITLES</u>

A. ARNOLD SCHOENBERG (1974-1951)
   1. Pioneer of the atonal style
   2. Influenced by music of Brahms and Wagner
   3. A painter, involved with Expressionism
   4. Expressionist style in music
      a. Mood changes
      b. Contrasts of tension and relaxation, loudness and softness, dense and sparse sounds
      c. Sprechstimme (<u>Pierrot Lunaire</u>)
      d. Klangfarbenmelodie
   5. Serialism (Dodecaphony)
      a. Twelve-tone row (series)
         (1) Forms: Original, Retrograde Inversion ,
         (2) Hauptstimme, Nebenstimme
      b. Example: <u>Suite for Piano</u> (Opus 25)
B. ALBAN BERG (1885-1935)
   1. Disciple of Schoenberg
   2. Serial technique with lyrical accent
   3. Examples:
      a. Opera: <u>Wozzeck</u>
      b. Violin Concerto
      c. <u>Lyric Suite</u>
C. ANTON VON WEBERN (1883-1945)
   1. Disciple of Schoenberg
   2. Melody merges with harmony
   3. Octave displacement is common
   4. Lean, sparse style
   5. Economy of means (short works)
   6. Pointillism

7. Example:
   a. Symphony (Opus 21)

COMPLETE THE FOLLOWING:

1. In the twentieth century, some composers were deliberately abandoning tonal centers in their music, a style which would come to be known as _____.

2. The first, and most important, pioneer of the above style was the composer _____.

3. Two 19th-Century composers who greatly influenced the musical style of the above composer were _____ and _____.

4. Schoenberg's early works are in the post-romantic style, chromatic, but still basically _____.

5. Schoenberg, who was also a painter as well as a composer was associated with the _____ movement in German painting, a term which also came to be used to describe his musical style.

6. A Schoenberg technique used by him in his vocal music is known as _____ or "speaking voice," in which the singer only sings approximate pitches.

7. A Schoenberg innovation in which each note of a melody is given to a different instrument is known as _____ _____, or "tone-color melody."

8. Schoenberg worked out a new method of organizing atonal harmony called _____, or _____, in which the twelve pitches of the _____ scale are arranged in a desired order and then used serially in that order.

9. The series of pitches in the above style are usually referred to as a _____ _____, and can be used in four different forms: _____, _____, _____ and _____.

10. In addition to being a composer and artist, Schoenberg was also an important _____.

11. One of Schoenberg's most famous pupils was Alban _____, who used Schoenberg's atonal and twelve-tone techniques, but tempered them with a strong sense of _____.

12. To indicate the principal part and secondary part of a musical phrase in the serial technique, the German terms _____ and _____ are used.

13. Another of Schoenberg's most famous pupils was Anton von _____, whose approach to atonality and dodeca-phony was more _____ in its approach.

14. Because of the economy of means in Webern's style, his pieces are exceptionally _____.

15. Webern utilized a compositional technique known by the painting term _____, in which a single note or very short motive is followed immediately by another one in another part in a higher or lower register.

WHICH OF THE THREE MAJOR ATONAL/SERIAL COMPOSERS
WROTE EACH OF THE FOLLOWING WORKS:
SCHOENBERG (S), BERG (B), OR WEBERN (W)?

1. _____ Pierrot Lunaire
2. _____ Wozzeck
3. _____ Lyric Suite
4. _____ Symphony: Opus 21
5. _____ Moses and Aaron

ON THE FOLLOWING MUSIC STAVES WRITE OUT
A TONE ROW IN ITS FOUR POSSIBLE FORMS:

LISTENING STUDY GUIDE

EXAMPLE 1: SCHOENBERG: <u>PIERROT LUNAIRE: "MONDESTRUNKEN"</u>
SIDE 11, BAND 1

1. The vocal technique used in this song is known as:
   a. Falsetto
   b. Sprechstimme
2. The accompaniment is played by a(n):
   a. Orchestra
   b. Chamber Ensemble
3. The language is:
   a. French
   b. German
4. The instrumental lines are primarily:
   a. Conjunct
   b. Disjunct
4. The harmony of this song is:
   a. Bitonal
   b. Atonal

EXAMPLE 2: SCHOENBERG: <u>SUITE FOR PIANO, OPUS 25:</u>
FIRST MOVEMENT
SIDE 11, BAND 2

1. The harmonic structure of this piece is:
   a. Modal
   b. Dodecaphonic
2. The tempo of this piece is
   a. Fast
   b. Slow
3. The texture is both contrapuntal and
   a. Monophonic
   b. Chordal
4. The form of this piece is:
   a. Sonata
   b. Free
5. The meter of this piece is very clear-cut.
   a. True
   b. False

EXAMPLE 3: BERG: <u>LYRIC SUITE: FIRST MOVEMENT:</u>
SIDE 11, BAND 3

1. The performing group is a:
   a. String Quartet
   b. Small Orchestra
2. The meter is essentially:
   a. Duple
   b. Triple
3. The harmonic structure is:
   a. Tonal
   b. Atonal

123

4. The melodic lines are extremely:
   a. Conjunct
   b. Disjunct
5. The form is:
   a. Binary
   b. Ternary

CHAPTER 28

Music in the Later Twentieth Century

A. THE EARLY POSTWAR YEARS (WORLD WAR II)
   1. Expansion of Serialism
      a. Total serialization
      b. Composers, Works:
         (1) Pierre Boulez (1925-   )
             (a) Le Marteau sans maitre
         (2) Karlheinz Stockhausen (1928-   )
             (a) Serial treatment of density,
                 register, tempo changes
             (b) Zeitmasse
         (3) Igor Stravinsky (1882-1971)
             (a) Late works only
             (b) Cantata, Movements for Piano and
                 Orchestra
         (4) Milton Babbit (1916-   )
             a. Use of intervals of duration
             b. Composition for Four Instruments
B. ELECTRONIC MUSIC
   1. Edgar Varese (1883-1965), a pioneer in the area
   2. Musique Concrete (Tape Music)
      a. Vladimir Ussachevsky (1911-   )
         (1) Of Wood and Brass
   3. Synthesized Sounds
      a. Oscillators, Synthesizers
      b. Columbia-Princeton Electronic Music Center
      c. Use of Computers
      d. Mario Davidovsky (1934-   )
         (1) Synchronisms No. 1

C. NEW SONORITIES WITH TRADITIONAL INSTRUMENTS
  1. New flute techniques
     a. Percussive sounds
  2. Prepared Piano
        (1) John Cage (1912-   )
  3. New string techniques
     a. Tapping the instrument
     b. Unstructured glissandos
     c. Rapid pizzicatos
     d. Krzysztof Penderecki (1933-   )
        (1) Polymorphia
  4. New percussion techniques
     a. Stravinsky: Les Noces, L'Histoire du Soldat
     b. Varese: Ionisation (all percussion)
  5. New vocal techniques
     a. Sprechstimme
        (1) Schoenberg: Pierrot Lunaire
     b. Luciano Berio (1925-   ): Circles
     c. George Crumb (1929-   )
        (1) Madrigals, Book IV
D. NEW PRINCIPLES OF STRUCTURE
  1. Chance Music (Aleatoric)
     a. Indeterminancy
     b. John Cage: Music of Changes
     c. Earle Brown (1926-   ): 25 Pages
        (1) Time notation
  2. Metric modulation
     a. Elliott Carter (1908-   )
        (1) Double Concerto for Piano and
            Harpsichord
  3. Minimalism
     a. Terry Riley (1935-   )
     b. Steve Reich (1936-   )
     c. Philip Glass (1937-   )
        (1) Einstein on the Beach
        (2) Modern Love Waltz
E. INCREASING ROLE FOR WOMEN IN MUSIC
  1. Margaret Hillis (1921-   ): Choral conductor
  2. Sarah Caldwell (1928-   ): Opera conductor
  3. Thea Musgrave (1928-   ): Composer

COMPLETE THE FOLLOWING:

1. Just before and during World War II, a number of important
   European composers, including _____,
   _____, _____ and _____.

2. After World War II, the City of _____ again
   became a center of creative musical activity, and many
   avant-garde composers went there to study with _____
   _____.

3. The above composer was greatly influenced by the rhythm
    of _____ music and _____ music,
    and many of his works contain rhythmic _____.

4. The twelve-tone system of composition expanded to include
    the serialization of more than one, or all, elements of
    music, a concept known as _____ _____.

5. A student of Messiaen who would later become a major 20th-
    Century composer, Pierre _____, extended
    the twelve-tone concept to include a _____

6. A German student of Messiaen, Karlheinz _____
    serialized density, register and tempo changes in his
    music.

7. Igor Stravinsky's first atonal work, entitled _____
    _____, was written in _____ a year
    after Schoenberg's death.

8. An important American composer and theorist of serial
    music was _____.

9. An early form of electronic music produced in France was
    known as _____ _____ _____, usually
    referred to as _____ _____ in
    America.

10. An early French pioneer of electronic music was the com-
    poser Edgar _____.

11. Electronic music was produced by means of _____
    and sound _____.

12. The first major center for electronic music in the United
    States was the _____ Electronic
    Music Center in New York.

13. A further innovation in the creation of electronic music
    was the use of the _____.

14. An innovative Argentinian/American composer of electronic
    music was Mario _____.

15. New techniques in writing for the flute were pioneered in
    the work "Density 21.5," by _____.

16. New techniques in writing for the piano were pioneered by
    the American composer _____, who muted
    the strings of the piano with pieces of woodk metal,
    rubber and glass in a technique known as _____
    piano.

17. New techniques in writing for strings were pioneered by the Polish composer _____.

18. New techniques in writing for percussion were pioneered by Stravinsky, in his works _____ and _____ _____.

19. New vocal techniques, after the pioneering work done by Schoenberg with Sprechstimme, were produced by the composer Luciano _____ in his work entitled _____.

20. Another composer who did innovative work in developing new vocal techniques was George _____ especially in his collection of _____, and in his song cycle entitled _____.

21. The division of the octave into more than twelve portions created a style of composition known as _____ _____, a pioneer of which was the eccentric American composer, Harry _____.

22. John Cage created a new concept of composition which was totally unstructured, a music which came to be known as _____ music, or _____ _____ often formally referred to as _____ music.

23. One of Cage's first major works in the above style is entitled "Music of _____."

24. A colleague of Cage, Earle Brown, included in his work entitled "25 Pages" a new method of notation known as _____ notation.

25. An American composer who has encouraged young composers to look for new approaches to musical structure is Elliott _____.

26. A contemporary compositional technique which involves numerous repetitions of tiny motives and groups of motives is known as _____.

27. The above style was greatly influenced by jazz, _____ music, and ideas of Erik Satie and _____.

28. Two important composers of minimalist music are Terry _____ and Phillip _____.

29. Due to the development of the long-playing record and tape, new music has acquired a degree of _____ _____.

30. Three important women in 20th-Century music are the choral conductor Margaret _____, the opera conductor Sarah _____ and the composer Thea _____.

<u>WHO WROTE EACH OF THE FOLLOWING LATE 20TH-CENTURY COMPOSITIONS?</u>

1. Ancient Voices of Children
   _____

2. Music of Changes
   _____

3. Composition for Four Instruments
   _____

4. Synchronisms
   _____

5. Polymorphia
   _____

6. L'Histoire du Soldat
   _____

7. Le Marteau sans Maitre
   _____

8. Of Wood and Brass
   _____

9. Zeitmasse
   _____

10. Twenty-Five Pages
    _____

<u>LISTENING STUDY GUIDE</u>

EXAMPLE 1:   DAVIDOVSKY: <u>SYNCHRONISMS #1</u>:
                          <u>SIDE 12, HAND 1</u>

1. This work is written for electronic tape and:
   a. Clarinet
   b. Flute
2. The title <u>Synchronism</u> implies:
   a. The relationship of tonalities
   b. The relationship of the solo instrument and the electronic tape
3. The melody is essentially:
   a. Conjunct
   b. Disjunct
4. The form of this piece is essentially

           a. Binary
           b. Ternary
    5. The meter is:
           a. Duple
           b. Triple
           c. Not apparent

EXAMPLE 2: PENDERECKI: POLYMORPHIA:
                    SIDE 11, BAND 6
    1. This work is set for:
           a. Full orchestra
           b. String orchestra
    2. The texture of the opening measures is:
           a. Monophonic
           c. Homophonic
    3. A prominent aspect of this piece is:
           a. Arpeggios
           b. Tone Clusters
    4. The form is:
           a. Highly structured
           b. Free
    5. This piece is entirely dissonant throughout.
           a. True
           b. False

EXAMPLE 3: CRUMB: MADRIGALS, BOOK IV:
                "POR QUE NACI ENTRE ESPEJOS?"
                    SIDE 12, BAND 2
    1. The vocal soloist is a:
           a. Soprano
           b. Contralto
    2. A melodic feature of this song is the use of:
           a. Arpeggios
           b. Glissandi
    3. In addition to singing, the singer also:
           a. Hums
           b. Whispers
    4. Unusual sounds are heard from the:
           a. Flute
           b. Cello
    5. The melodic line is generally disjunct and:
           a. Lyrical
           b. Detached

EXAMPLE 4: GLASS: MODERN LOVE WALTZ:
                    SIDE 12, BAND 3
    1. This piece is an example of what contemporary style?
           a. Minimalism
           b. Pointillism
    2. A contemporary instrument heard here is the:
           a. Electric Guitar
           b. Electric Piano

3. The bass line features:
   a. Imitative techniques
   b. Arpeggiated chords
4. The harmonic structure is:
   a. Very complex
   b. Very simple
5. The meter is:
   a. Duple
   b. Triple

CHAPTER 29

American Popular Music

A. SOURCES OF POPULAR MUSIC
    1. Anglo-American Folk Music
        a. Conjunct melodies, chordal accompaniments
        b. Phrases of equal length
        c. Symmetrical, strophic form
        d. Homophonic texture
        e. Ballads
        f. Occupational songs
        g. Instrumental music
            (1) Square Dances
            (2) Marches
        h. Play songs, love songs, lullabies
    2. Folk Music from other Nations
        a. France: Alouette, Frere Jacques
        b. Germany: O Tannenbaum
    3. Folk song singers:
        a. Joan Baez (1941-   )
        b. Pete Seeger (1919-   )
    4. Black Folk Music
        a. Field Hollers, Group Work Songs
        b. Ring Shouts, Song Sermons
        c. Lining out
        d. The Blues
            (1) Blue Notes
            (2) I-IV-V harmony
            (3) 12 bars, AAB structure
            (4) Bessie Smith (1894-1937) and "Ma"
                Rainey (1886-1939)
        e. Black Spirituals, Gospel Hymns

        f. White performers in blackface
            (1) Minstrel Shows, Vaudeville
    B. JAZZ
        1. Syncopated rhythm, improvisation
        2. Ragtime piano style
            a. Scott Joplin (1868-1917)
        3. New Orleans (Storyville)
        4. Early Jazz Styles
            a. "Jelly Roll" Morton (1885-1941)
            b. Louis Armstrong (c. 1898-1971)
                (1) West End Blues
            c. Bix Beiderbecke (1901-1931)
                (1) First major white jazz musician
        5. Jazz combos
    C. SWING
        1. The Big Band Era
            a. Written arrangements
            b. Fletcher Henderson (1898-1952)
                (1) King Porter Stomp (Benny Goodman)
            c. "Duke" Ellington (1899-1974)
    D. BOP (BEBOP)
        1. Rhythmic diversity, formal unpredictability
        2. Charlie Parker (1920-1955)
            a. Ornithology
    E. JAZZ IN THE LATER 20TH CENTURY
        1. Cool Jazz
            a. More lyrical melodic approach to jazz
            b. Miles Davis (1926-   )
        2. Third Stream Jazz
            a. Combining jazz and traditional music
                (1) Gunther Schuller (1925-   )
    F. BROADWAY AND MUSICAL COMEDY
        1. Operetta imported from Europe
            a. Victor Herbert (1859-1924)
            b. Sigmund Romberg (1887-1951)
        2. George M. Cohan (1878-1942)
            a. Established the Musical Comedy concept
        3. Other notable composers in this area
            a. Irving Berlin (1888-   )
            b. Jerome Kern (1885-1945)
            c. Richard Rodgers (1902-1979)
                (1) With Oscar Hammerstein as lyricist
            d. Leonard Bernstein (1918-   )
            e. Stephen Sondheim (1930-   )
    G. COUNTRY AND WESTERN MUSIC
        1. Sung in high-pitched nasal style
        2. Accompanied by guitar or banjo
        3. Grand Ole Opry
        4. Western Swing Style
        5. Country Blues
            a. Hank Williams (1921-1953)
        6. Pop Country Music and Bluegrass

133

H. ROCK MUSIC
    1. Rockabilly
    2. Rock and Roll
        a. Chuck Berry (1926-   )
        b. Elvis Presley (1935-1977)
    3. Teen Rock: Pat Boone (1934-   )
    4. The Beatles
    5. The Rolling Stones
    6. Folk-Protest Songs (1960s)
    7. Raga Rock, Acid Rock, British Progressive
    8. Rock Operas: Hair, Tommy
    9. Soul Music (Black orientation)
   10. Disco
   11. Punk Rock, New Wave Rock, Heavy Metal Rock

COMPLETE THE FOLLOWING:

1. American popular music in American encompasses _____
    music, _____ music, _____, _____
    and _____.

2. The two major folk music traditions in America are
    _____-_____ folk music and _____
    folk music.

3. Much American folk music is rooted in which two European
    countries? _____ and _____.

4. Folk music is passed on _____ from one person
    or generation to another.

5. The rhythm and meter of folk music is usually derived to
    some extent from the _____ of the songs.

6. An important prototype of the Anglo-American folk song is
    the English _____, which is typically comprised
    of several _____ with a recurrent.

7. Many folk songs had either no accompaniment, or were sup-
    ported by simple accompaniment of a _____,
    _____ or _____.

8. Instrumental folk music was usually written for activities
    such as _____ or _____.

9. Other European countries whose folk music has found its
    way into American folk music are _____,
    _____, _____ and _____,
    among many others.

10. Black folk music is derived from two types of songs sung
    by African slaves, the _____ _____ and the
    and the _____ _____ song.

11. A type of black folk music involving a shuffling dance
    with chanting and handclapping is known as the _____
    _____.

12. A method of teaching new songs, was for a leader to sing
    one line of a song at a time, the assembled group repeat-
    ing that line after him, a technique known as _____
    _____.

13. A major form of Black folk music relates to the singing of
    a lament about the hard life of slavery, a style of sing-
    ing known as the _____, a term which has come to
    refer to sadness in the American dialect.

14. The religious counterpart of the above vocal form was
    known as the _____.

15. A Protestant revival movement in the United States in the
    1950s led to a black and/or white type of sacred song
    known as _____ _____.

16. A kind of popular musical entertainment which had whites
    masquerading as blacks was known as the _____
    _____ show, an entertainment which lost its
    racist aspects in the early 20th Century and came to be
    known as _____.

17. Most of the various types of Black folk music combined in
    the late years of the 19th and early years of the 20th
    centuries in a uniquely American form of music known as
    _____.

18. The above musical style is distinguished by its emphasis
    on rhythm, especially _____, and its
    frequent use of _____.

19. An early form of a piano style of jazz was known as _____
    _____, one of its earliest pioneers being _____
    _____.

20. The American city where jazz was born and nurtured is
    "red light" district of that city known as _____
    _____.

21. Important early Jazz figures include Buddy _____
    "Jelly Roll" _____, "King" _____ and
    the legendary Louis _____.

135

22. The first major White jazz musician was Bix _____
    _____.

23. Small jazz ensembles are usually referred to as _____
    _____.

24. The 1930s is generally referred to as the _____
    _____ era in American popular music, playing a
    style of music known as _____, and pioneered by
    such bandleaders as Fletcher _____ and
    "Duke" _____.

25. A feature of the above style of the 1930s is that although
    jazz groups improvised what they played, these groups
    played from written _____.

26. An important form of jazz during the 1940s was known as
    _____, two of its leading performers being
    Charlie _____ and "Dizzy" _____.

27. Jazz in the later 20th Century was often referred to as
    _____ jazz, one of its major performers being
    Miles _____.

28. A combination of classical music and jazz came to be known
    as _____ _____, pioneered by _____
    _____ and _____.

29. A musical/dramatic form which made its debut in the United
    States during the late 19th Century was _____,
    especially involving the works of two European composers,
    _____ and _____.

30. The first major development in American Musical Theater
    was the product of the Irish/American showman and producer
    George M. _____, producing a form which came to
    be known as musical _____.

31. Other important composers in the field of the American
    Musical Theater were _____, _____,
    _____ and _____.

32. One of the earliest sources of Country/Western music was
    the Nashville weekly radio show entitled _____
    _____.

33. In the American Southwest, a style of popular music known
    as _____ _____ emerged derived from
    the music of the labor camps and oil fields known as
    _____ _____.

34. A popular type of country/western instrumental music, dominated by the country fiddler, came to be known as _____ music.

35. The early appearance of Rock and Roll in the 1950s was coupled to the country/western style in a type of music known as _____ music.

36. A major figure of the early development of Rock and Roll was the superstar performer _____.

37. A significant impact was made on American Rock and Roll with the "invasion" of the music group from England known as the _____ in the early 1960s.

38. Another English group who impacted on the evolution of the American Rock style was the group known as the _____ - _____.

39. Rock made incursions into the field of the Broadway theatrical world with the appearance of rock _____.

40. In addition to Soul Music and Disco Music, other types of music to make inroads into the Rock scene in America of the 1970s and 1980s are _____ rock, _____ _____ rock and _____ _____ rock.

<u>INDICATE WHICH AREA OF AMERICAN POPULAR MUSIC THE FOLLOWING INDIVIDUALS WERE MOST CLOSELY ASSOCIATED WITH:</u>

1. Roy Acuff   _____
2. Charlie Parker   _____
3. Jerome Kern   _____
4. Bob Dylan   _____
5. Scott Joplin   _____
6. Bessie Smith   _____
7. Louis Armstrong   _____
8. Gunther Schuller   _____
9. Duke Ellington   _____
10. Little Richard   _____

<u>LISTENING STUDY GUIDE</u>

EXAMPLE 1: WILLIAMS/OLIVER/ARMSTRONG: <u>WEST END BLUES</u>
                                        <u>SIDE 12, BAND 4</u>
  1. The piece begins with a solo for:
        a. Voice
        b. Trumpet

2. The melodic line features:
   a. Sprechstimme
   b. Improvisation
3. The tonality is primarily:
   a. Major
   b. Minor
4. How many times is the 12-bar blues formula presented:
   a. Two
   b. Three
   c. Five
5. The meter is:
   a. Duple
   b. Triple

EXAMPLE 2: MORTON/HENDERSON: <u>King Porter Stomp</u>:
                                  <u>SIDE 12, BAND 5</u>
1. The performing group is a:
   a. Small combo
   b. Large band
2. The meter is:
   a. Duple
   b. Triple
3. The tonality is:
   a. Major
   b. Minor
4. The rhythm section is comprised of piano, bass drum and:
   a. Guitar
   b. Xylophone
5. The melody dominates throughout.
   a. True
   b. False

EXAMPLE 3: HARRIS/PARKER: <u>ORNITHOLOGY</u>:
                                  <u>SIDE 12, BAND 6</u>
1. The style of this piece is:
   a. Cool Jazz
   b. Bebop
2. The two featured wind instruments are trumpet and:
   a. Clarinet
   b. Saxophone
3. The meter is:
   a. Duple
   b. Triple
4. The form is:
   a. Free
   b. Sectional
5. The tonality is:
   a. Major
   b. Minor

CHAPTER 30

Aspects of Music in Some Non-Western Cultures

A. MUSIC OF AFRICA
    1. Music an essential part of daily life
    2. Music and dance serve as unifying forces
    3. Bantu Music
        a. Central Africa (Sub-Saharan)
        b. Bantu languages are "tonal" in nature
        c. Instruments can be used to convey verbal
            meanings
        d. Short melodic phrases
        e. Responsorial singing, with improvised
            variations on the basic phrase.
        f. Harmonic techniques
            (1) Parallel motion
            (2) Drone notes
B. MUSIC OF THE AMERICAN INDIAN
    1. Music of the Plains
        a. Wide-ranging melodies
        b. Complex, changing rhythms
        c. First half of song sung with meaningless
            syllables, high-pitched voices
        d. Remainder of text can be varied
        e. Incomplete repetition (ABCBC or AABCABC)
        f. Ceremonial dances
    2. Pueblo Music
        a. More complex than Plains Indian music
            (1) Longer, more varied
            (2) Six- or seven-note scales
        b. Low, growling voices
    3. Invit Music
        a. Northwest coastal region

        b.   Rhythmically complex, variety of contrasting
             accents and meters
        c.   Undulating melodies, recitative style
   C. MUSIC OF INDIA
        1. Ragas
        2. Talas
        3. Drone notes or drone chords
        4. Improvisational
        5. Voice is primary
        6. Sitar, tambura, tabla
   D. MUSIC OF CHINA
        1. Music believed to be related to the cosmos
             a.   To imitate and uphold the proper harmony
                  between heaven and earth
        2. Ya-yueh and Su-yueh Music
        3. Use of pentatonic scales
        4. Chinese Opera
        5. Hsiao, Sheng, P'i-p'a and Ch''in

COMPLETE THE FOLLOWING:

1. Some of the many functions of music in many cultures are
    as part of _____ rites, _____, and a
    multitude of different types of _____ as
    well as being performed solely for popular _____.

2. In many African cultures, music and dance serve as _____
    _____ forcesk pervading all aspects of life.

3. The music of the Bantu-speaking peoples of _____
    Africa is in many ways representative of the musical tra-
    ditions of _____ Africa.

4. An important aspect of Bantu music is the _____
    aspect of Bantu languages, in which the meaning of a word
    depends partly on the _____ at which the sylla-
    bles of the word are spoken.

5. The call-and-response aspect of much African music is
    referred to formally as _____ singing.

6. Bantu songs are often sung in _____ motion,
    and make frequent use of _____, often with one
    voice holding a long _____ note.

7. The complexity of African music is quite remarkable, often
    combining several rhythms at the same time, creating a
    kind of rhythmic _____.

8. In the traditional songs of the Plains Indians of America,
    melodies cover a wide _____, rhythm is _____

and changing, and voice quality is very tense and _____ _____.

9. Musically-accompanied ceremonial _____ play an important part in the lives of the American Plains Indians.

10. The text of the first half of many American Indian songs is frequently made up of _____ syllables.

11. The musical form of the music of the Plains Indians is usually referred to as _____ repetition.

12. The songs of the Pueblo Indians are much more complex than the songs of the _____ Indians, longer and more varied, and based on _____ or _____ note scales.

13. The songs of the Invit Indians of the American Northwest are often sung in a declamatory or _____ style of singing.

14. The music of India is based on melodic formulas called _____ and rhythmic formulas called _____.

15. Indian music usually features a drone _____ or _____ in performance.

16. The voice is primary in Indian music, for it is thought to be the most perfect blending of the _____ and the _____.

17. The principal stringed instrument of India is the _____, another important stringed instrument being the _____.

18. The principal percussion instrument used in Indian music is the _____.

19. The two traditional categories of Chinese music are the refined _____ style and the more common _____ style.

20. The basic scale of much Chinese music is the _____, or five-note scale.

141

LISTENING STUDY GUIDE

EXAMPLE 1: <u>WORK SONG FROM BURUNDI:</u>
SIDE 12, BAND 7
1. The style of the music is:
   a. Responsorial
   b. Antiphonal
2. The singers are:
   a. Male
   b. Female
   c. Mixed
3. The essential direction of the melodic line is:
   a. Ascending
   b. Descending
4. The rhythm is:
   a. Constantly changing
   b. Repetitive
5. The essential texture is:
   a. Monophonic
   b. Homophonic

EXAMPLE 2: <u>IBIHUBI:</u>
SIDE 12, BAND 8
1. This piece is played entirely on:
   a. Strings
   b. Drums
2. The form of this piece is:
   a. Highly structured
   b. Free
3. The sounds of the various instruments are:
   a. Similar
   b. Different
4. How many layers of texture are evident?
   a. Two
   b. Three
   c. Four
5. The music maintains a basic beat.
   a. True
   b. False

EXAMPLE 3: <u>WILD GEESE LANDING ON THE SAND BEACH:</u>
SIDE 12, BAND 9
1. The opening motive features:
   a. Octave leaps
   b. A distonic, conjunct line
2. The melodic line is heard in which scale?
   a. Chromatic
   b. Pentatonic
3. The rhythmic structure is:
   a. Tightly constructed
   b. Free

4. The melodic motives are:
   a. Constantly changing
   b. Often repeated
   c. Both of the above
5. The final note of the piece is:
   a. Held out
   b. Repeated several times

ANSWERS

CHAPTER ONE

 (1) Pitch
 (2) Notes
 (3) Staff
 (4) Melody
 (5) Disjunct melody
 (6) Conjunct melody
 (7) Contrast, repetition
 (8) Phrase
 (9) Rhythm
(10) Meter
(11) Duple
(12) Triple
(13) Measures
(14) Tempo
(15) Accelerando, ritardando, rallentando
             ****

 (1) S   (6) S
 (2) VF   (7) VF
 (3) M   (8) M
 (4) VS   (9) VS
 (5) F   (10) VF

CHAPTER TWO

- (1) Harmony
- (2) Interval
- (3) Chord
- (4) Accompaniment
- (5) Consonant, Dissonant
- (6) Twelve
- (7) Major
- (8) Tonic
- (9) 3rd-4th, 7th-8th
- (10) Tonic chord
- (11) Subdominant
- (12) Dominant
- (13) Cadence
- (14) Authentic
- (15) Plagal
- (16) Accidental
- (17) Modulation
- (18) Texture
- (19) Monophonic
- (20) Polyphonic
- (21) Imitative
- (22) Nonimitative
- (23) Homophonic
- (24) Arpeggios
- (25) Mixture

****

- (1) 3rd
- (2) 5th
- (3) 7th
- (4) 6th
- (5) 2nd
- (6) 4th
- (7) 5th
- (8) 2nd
- (9) 8ve
- (10) 6th

****

- (1) E-G-B
- (2) A-C-E
- (3) G-B-D
- (4) B-D-F
- (5) F-A-C

CHAPTER THREE

```
 (1) Timbre
 (2) Voice
 (3) Larynx
 (4) Chordophone
 (5) Aerophone
 (6) Membranophone
 (7) Idiophone
 (8) Orchestration
 (9) Dynamics
(10) Left
```

****

```
     Pianissimo
     Piano
     Mezzopiano
     Mezzoforte
     Forte
     Fortissimo
```

****

```
 (1) W      (6) P
 (2) B      (7) W
 (3) S      (8) S
 (4) P      (9) P
 (5) W     (10) B
```

CHAPTER FOUR

```
 (1) Form, structure, shape
 (2) Repetition, Contrast
 (3) Motives
 (4) Phrases
 (5) Sections
 (6) Stanzas
 (7) Strophic
 (8) Ternary
 (9) Binary
(10) Rondo
(11) Variation
(12) Free
(13) Movements
(14) Renaissance
(15) Romantic
```
          ****
```
    Mediaeval
    Renaissance
    Classical
    Baroque
    Romantic
    Twentieth Century
```
          ****
```
 (1) ABA
 (2) ABACABA
 (3) AB
 (4) A A1 A2 A3 A4
```

147

CHAPTER FIVE

 (1) Pitch, duration
 (2) Staff, Five
 (3) Ledger
 (4) Clef
 (5) Treble Clef, Bass Clef
 (6) Great
 (7) Alto, Tenor, Middle C
 (8) Sharp, half-step
 (9) Flat, half-step
(10) Sharps, Flats
(11) Twelve
(12) Key Signature
(13) Major, Minor
(14) 3rd-7th, 2nd-5th
(15) Natural
(16) Accidentals
(17) Duration
(18) Beams
(19) Tie, Dot
(20) Rests
(21) Measures, Bar
(22) One
(23) Beats, Measure
(24) 4/4
(25) Metronome
      ****
 (1) Gb   (6) C#
 (2) C   (7) Ab
 (3) G#   (8) Bb
 (4) B   (9) Eb
 (5) F   (10) E

CHAPTER SIX

(1) 5th
(2) Church
(3) Religion
(4) Vespers
(5) Mass, Ordinary, Proper
(6) Kyrie Eleison, Gloria, Credo
     Sanctus/Benedictus, Agnus Dei
(7) Gregorian Chant
(8) Neumes
(9) Mode, Authentic, Plagal
(10) Melismatic
(11) Syllabic
(12) Requiem Mass
(13) Troubadours, Trouveres
(14) Organum
(15) Tenor, Duplum
(16) Leonin
(17) Magnus Liber Organi
(18) Perotin
(19) Motet
(20) Ars Nova, Phillipe de Vitry
(21) Machaut
(22) Messe de Notre Dame
(23) Rondeau, Virelai, Ballade, Lai
(24) Madrigal, Caccia, Ballata
(25) Landini
     ****
(1) Kyrie Eleison
(2) Gloria
(3) Credo
(4) Sanctus/Benedictus
(5) Agnus Dei
     ****

(1) D	(5) E
(2) F	(6) G
(3) G	(7) F
(4) D	(8) E

     ****

LISTENING

EXAMPLE 1:	EXAMPLE 2:	EXAMPLE 3:	EXAMPLE 4:
(1) A	(1) B	(1) A	(1) A
(2) B	(2) B	(2) B	(2) A
(3) B	(3) A	(3) A	(3) C
(4) A	(4) A	(4) A	(4) B
(5) B	(5) A	(5) A	(5) A

   (1) Italy
   (2) England
   (3) 15th, 16th
   (4) Four
   (5) Imitation
   (6) Dissonance
   (7) Text Painting
   (8) Dufay
   (9) Ockeghem
(10) Josquin
(11) Isaac
(12) Luther
(13) Chorale
(14) Trent
(15) Lassus
(16) Palestrina
(17) Gabrieli
(18) Byrd
(19) 1501, Venice,
     Odhecaton, Petrucci
(20) Madrigal
(21) Gesualdo
(22) Monteverdi
(23) Morley
(24) Consort, Pavane-Galliard
(25) Harpsichord
        ****

  (1) M   (6) R
  (2) R   (7) R
  (3) M   (8) M
  (4) M   (9) R
  (5) R   (10) R
      ****

  (1) Josquin
  (2) Isaac
  (3) Luther
  (4) Monteverdi
  (5) Morley
      ****

LISTENING

EXAMPLE 1:	EXAMPLE 2:	EXAMPLE 3:	EXAMPLE 4:
(1) A	(1) A	(1) B	(1) B
(2) B	(2) B	(2) C	(2) C
(3) A	(3) A	(3) A	(3) B
(4) B	(4) C	(4) A	(4) A
(5) A	(5) B	(5) B	(5) B

 (1) Portuguese, Italian, Barocci
 (2) Decadence
 (3) France, Sun
 (4) El Greco, Rembrandt
 (5) Afffections
 (6) Camerata, Bardi
 (7) Stile Rappresentativo
 (8) Monody
 (9) Ornaments
(10) Recitative, Aria
(11) Bel Canto
(12) Arioso
(13) Sequence
(14) Tonality
(15) Progression
(16) Equal Temperament
(17) Basso Continuo
(18) Figured Bass, Realization
(19) Imitative Counterpoin
(20) Organ, Clavichord, Harpsichord
(21) Violin Family
(22) Movements
(23) Concertato
(24) Terraced
(25) Psalter, Common, Regular

****

STRING	WOODWIND	BRASS
Violin	Flute	Trumpet
Viola	Oboe	Horn
Cello	Bassoon	Trombone

****

 (1) R   (6) B
 (2) B   (7) B
 (3) B   (8) B
 (4) R   (9) R
 (5) R   (10) B

CHAPTER NINE

(1) Caccini, Euridice
(2) Nuove Musiche
(3) Soprano, Continuo
(4) Opera, Orfeo
(5) Chromaticism
(6) Recitativo Secco,
    Recitativo Accompagnato
(7) Strophic Bass
(8) 1637, Venice
(9) Scarlatti
(10) Opera Buffa
(11) Lully
(12) Purcell, Dido and Aeneas
(13) Handel, Julius Caesar
(14) Castrati
(15) Cantata
(16) Scarlatti, Schuetz, Buxtehude
(17) J.S.Bach
(18) Oratorio
(19) Cavalieri, Handel, Messiah
(20) Missa Brevis, Bach
    ****
(1) Handel
(2) Monteverdi
(3) Handel
(4) Purcell
(5) Schuetz
    ****

LISTENING

EXAMPLE 1:	EXAMPLE 2:	EXAMPLE 3:	EXAMPLE 4:
(1) A	(1) B	(1) B	(1) A
(2) B	(2) B	(2) A	(2) A
(3) B	(3) B	(3) B	(3) B
(4) A	(4) A	(4) B	(4) A
(5) B	(5) B	(5) A	(5) C

CHAPTER TEN

  (1) Orchestra, Instrumental
  (2) Solo, Trio
  (3) Church, Chamber
  (4) Corelli
  (5) Scarlatti
  (6) France, Lully
  (7) Concerto Grosso,
      Conceertino, Ripieno
  (8) Solo, Torelli
  (9) Ritornello
 (10) Opus
 (11) Vivaldi, Venice
 (12) Fugue, Subject, Episodes
 (13) J.S.Bach, The Art of the Fugue
 (14) Well-Tempered Clavier
 (15) Sinfonias
 (16) Lully, Scarlatti
 (17) Suite
 (18) Ordre, Couperin
 (19) Partita
 (20) Toccata, Frescobaldi
      ****
  (1) Violin, Viola, Cello
  (2) Flute, Horn, Oboe
  (3) Harpsichord, Organ, Lute
  (4) Viol da Gamba, Cello, Bass
      ****

LISTENING

EXAMPLE 1:	EXAMPLE 2:	EXAMPLE 3:	EXAMPLE 4:
(1) B	(1) A	(1) B	(1) B
(2) A	(2) B	(2) B	(2) B
(3) B	(3) B	(3) B	(3) A
(4) B	(4) A	(4) A	(4) B
(5) A	(5) B	(5) B	(5) B

CHAPTER ELEVEN

 (1) 18th, 19th
 (2) Simplicity
 (3) J.S.Bach
 (4) Rococo, Couperin
 (5) Empfindsamer, C.P.E.Bach
 (6) Melody
 (7) Phrases
 (8) Variety
 (9) Harmony
(10) Dominant, Tonic
(11) Closely related, Major, Minor
(12) Homophonic
(13) 30, 40, String
(14) Mannheim, Stamitz
(15) Left, Right
(16) Sonata Cycle, Sonata,
     Symphony, Concerto
(17) Exposition, Development,
     Recapitulation
(18) Coda
(19) Rondo
(20) Ternary
(21) Variations
(22) Singing
(23) Billings
(24) Fasola, Shape-Note
(25) Hopkinson, "My Days Have
     Been so Wondrous Free"
     ****
 (1) String
 (2) Oboe, Bassoon
 (3) Clarinet
 (4) Trumpets, Horns
 (5) Timpani
     ****
 (1) C
 (2) B
 (3) B
 (4) C
 (5) C

CHAPTER TWELVE

 (1) Italian Overture
 (2) Suite
 (3) Minuet
 (4) Haydn
 (5) Four, Slow, Fast
 (6) Esterhazy, Servant
 (7) 104
 (8) London, Salomon
 (9) "Surprise"
(10) Father
(11) Austrian
(12) 27, 5
(13) Koechel
(14) Spontaneously
(15) Six

****

LISTENING

EXAMPLE 1:	EXAMPLE 2:	EXAMPLE 3:	EXAMPLE 4:
(1) B	(1) A	(1) B	(1) B
(2) A	(2) B	(2) B	(2) A
(3) A	(3) B	(3) A	(3) A
(4) B	(4) B	(4) B	(4) A
(5) B	(5) B	(5) A	(5) B

CHAPTER THIRTEEN

   (1) Bonn, Vienna
   (2) Organist
   (3) Nine
   (4) Trombone
   (5) Voices
   (6) "Pastoral"
   (7) Five
   (8) Deafness
   (9) "Eroica", Napoleon
  (10) Funeral March, Scherzo
  (11) Motive
  (12) Double Theme & Variations
  (13) Schiller
  (14) Three
  (15) Nine
       ****

LISTENING

EXAMPLE 1:	EXAMPLE 2:	EXAMPLE 3:	EXAMPLE 4:
(1) B	(1) B	(1) A	(1) B
(2) B	(2) B	(2) A	(2) A
(3) A	(3) B	(3) B	(3) B
(4) B	(4) A	(4) A	(4) A
(5) B	95) B	(5) A	(5) B

CHAPTER FOURTEEN

 (1) Orchestra
 (2) Violin
 (3) Cadenza
 (4) Three
 (5) Ritornello, Sonata
 (6) Exposition
 (7) Slow
 (8) Sonata, Rondo
 (9) Contrast, Theme, Tonality
(10) Four
(11) Piano
(12) Harpsichord, Violin
(13) Drama, Expressiveness
(14) Five
(15) One
         ****

LISTENING

     EXAMPLE 1:
         (1) A
         (2) A
         (3) B
         (4) B
         (5) A

157

CHAPTER FIFTEEN

  (1) Small, One, Conductor
  (2) String Quartet, Violins,
      Viola, Cello
  (3) Piano
  (4) Sonatas
  (5) Four, Symphony
  (6) Haydn
  (7) Divertimenti
  (8) Haydn, Second,
      National Anthem
  (9) 23
 (10) Experimentation
 (11) Lyrical
 (12) Piano, Piano
 (13) Four
 (14) Beethoven
 (15) Haydn, Mozart, Schubert
      ****

LISTENING

EXAMPLE 1:   EXAMPLE 2:
 (1) B   (1) B
 (2) A   (2) A
 (3) B   (3) A
 (4) A   (4) B
 (5) B   (5) A

CHAPTER SIXTEEN

 (1) Opera
 (2) Sing, Speak, Stylized
 (3) Soprano
 (4) Coloratura
 (5) Prima Donna
 (6) Mezzo-Soprano, Contralto
 (7) Tenor
 (8) Baritone, Bass
 (9) Trouser, Pants
(10) Secco, Accompagnato
(11) Ensembles
(12) Libretto
(13) Synopses
(14) Stage Director
(15) Haydn, Mozart, Gluck,
     Beethoven
(16) Opera Buffa, Singspiel
(17) Opera Seria, Idomeneo,
     La Clemenza di Tito
(18) The Marriage of Figaro,
     Don Giovanni
(19) Spoken
(20) Fidelio
(21) Da Ponte
(22) The Creation, The Seasons
(23) Lord Nelson
(24) Christ on the Mount of Olives
(25) Missa Solemnis
    ****

LISTENING

EXAMPLE 1:   EXAMPLE 2:
(1) A   (1) A
(2) A   (2) B
(3) B   (3) A
(4) B   (4) A
(5) A   (5) A

 (1) Individual, Subjective
 (2) Rousseau, Inidividual Enjoyment
 (3) Industrial
 (4) Independence, Patronage,
     Individualism
 (5) Hero
 (6) Nature
 (7) Supernatural
 (8) Byron
 (9) Delacroix
(10) Painting, Poetry
(11) Inexpressible
(12) Longer, Irregular
(13) Chromaticism, Disjunct,
     Ornamentation
(14) Simple, Complex, Meters,
     Patterns, Meter
(15) Emotional
(16) Chromaticism
(17) Dissonant
(18) Chordal
(19) Small, Large
(20) Dynamic
(21) Piano
(22) Lieder, Chansons
(23) Symphony, Programmatic
(24) Symphonic Poem
(25) Opera, Play
(26) Secular, Longer, Imaginative
(27) Opera
(28) Emotions
(29) Thomas
(30) Foster, Gottschalk,
     Sousa, MacDowell
     ****

  (1) R   (6) C
  (2) C   (7) R
  (3) R   (8) C
  (4) C   (9) R
  (5) R   (10) R

CHAPTER EIGHTEEN

(1) Shorter, Structures
(2) Programmatic
(3) Character
(4) Mendelssohn, Brahms, Grieg,
    Albeniz, Rachmaninov
(5) Chopin, Liszt
(6) Legato, Sustaining
(7) Rubato
(8) Nocturnes, Field
(9) Melody, Chordal, Arpeggiated
(10) Etudes
(11) Mazurka, Polonaise, Waltz
(12) Ballade, Scherzo, Sonata
(13) George Sand
(14) 39
(15) Vienna, Paris
(16) Paganini
(17) Orchhestral
(18) Etudes
(19) Annees des Pelerinage
(20) Hungarian
    ****

LISTENING

EXAMPLE 1:
(1) B
(2) B
(3) B
(4) B
(5) A

EXAMPLE 2:
(1) A
(2) B
(3) B
(4) B
(5) B

CHAPTER NINETEEN

 (1) Chanson, Lied
 (2) Schubert
 (3) Cycle, <u>An Die Ferne Geliebte</u>
 (4) Piano, Poetry
 (5) Goethe, Schiller, Heine
 (6) Music, Voice
 (7) 600, 7
 (8) <u>Faust</u>, <u>Gretchen am Spinnrade</u>
 (9) <u>Erlkoenig</u>
(10) <u>Die Schoene Muellerin</u>
(11) 9, <u>The Trout</u>
(12) Schumann
(13) Piano, Critic
(14) Clara Wieck
(15) <u>Frauenliebe und Leben</u>,
    <u>Dichterliebe</u>
(16) Four, Piano, Cello,
    Violin, Piano
(17) Brahms
(18) Wagner
(19) Mahler, Wolf, Richard Strauss
(20) Berlioz, Faure, Debussy, Ravel
****

LISTENING

EXAMPLE 1:	EXAMPLE 2:
(1) B	(1) B
(2) B	(2) B
(3) B	(3) B
(4) B	(4) A
(5) B	(5) A

CHAPTER TWENTY

(1) Haydn, Mozart, Beethoven, Schubert
(2) "Unfinished"
(3) Liszt, Berlioz, Program
(4) Abstract, Mendelssohn, Brahms
(5) Dominant, Ninth
(6) Dense, Dynamics
(7) Timbre, Melody
(8) Five, Four
(9) Voices
(10) Classical, Romantic
(11) Four, Academic Festival, Tragic
(12) Schumann, Clara
(13) Clarinet, Horn, Cello
(14) Opera
(15) Piano, Violin
(16) Lieder
(17) St. Petersburg, Rubenstein
(18) Swan Lake, The Nutcracker
(19) Beethoven
(20) Six
(21) Emotional
(22) Franck
(23) Orchestra, Bruckner
(24) Mahler, Dvorak
(25) Solo, Orchestral
(26) Virtuoso
(27) Two, Piano
(28) Piano, Cello, Violin
(29) Piano, Violin
(30) Three

****

LISTENING

EXAMPLE 1:
(1) A
(2) B
(3) B
(4) B
(5) A

EXAMPLE 2:
(1) B
(2) B
(3) B
(4) A
(5) B

 (1) Arts
 (2) Cultural
 (3) Writers, Critics
 (4) Literary, Pictorial
 (5) Liszt
 (6) Sixth
 (7) Berlioz, Byron
 (8) Mussorgsky
 (9) Tchaikowsky, 1812
(10) Program, Poems, Overtures,
     Incidental
(11) Opera, Oratorio
(12) Mendelssohn, Tchaikovsky
(13) Incidental, Suite
(14) Midsummer Night's Dream
(15) Philosopher, Banker
(16) Piano, Organ, Violin
(17) Piano
(18) Five, Elijah, Violin
(19) Symphonie Fantastique
(20) Idee Fixe
(21) Large
(22) Timpani, Brass Bands
(23) Symphonic, Tone
(24) Liszt, Les Preludes
(25) Smetana, Tchaikovsky, Richard Strauss,
     Dukas, Sibelius
(26) Scordatura
(27) Ein Heldenleben, Sinfonia Domestica
(28) Juan, Quixote
(29) Operas
(30) Classical
             ****

LISTENING

EXAMPLE 1:	EXAMPLE 2:
(1) C	(1) B
(2) B	(2) A
(3) A	(3) B
(4) A	(4) B
(5) B	(5) B

 (1) <u>Don Giovanni</u>, <u>Fidelio</u>
 (2) French, Italian, German
 (3) Paris
 (4) Grand, Meyerbeer
 (5) Opera Comique, Offenbach
 (6) LYric, Thomas, Gounod
 (7) Bizet, <u>Carmen</u>
 (8) St.-Saens, Massenet
 (9) Music, Drama
(10) Rossini, <u>The Barber of Seville</u>
(11) Donizetti, Bellini
(12) <u>Nabucco</u>
(13) <u>Rigoletto</u>, <u>Il Trovatore</u>,
     <u>La Traviata</u>
(14) <u>Les Vepres Siciliennes</u>, <u>Don Carlos</u>
(15) <u>Aida</u>, Grand, Italian
(16) Otello, Falstaff
(17) Verismo
(18) Leoncavallo, Mascagni, <u>I Pagliacci</u>,
     <u>Cavalleria Rusticana</u>
(19) Puccini
(20) <u>Madame Butterfly</u>, <u>Turandot</u>
(21) Rome, Paris
(22) Weber, <u>Der Freischuetz</u>
(23) Wagner, Music Dramas
(24) <u>The Flying Dutchman</u>
(25) <u>Lohengrin</u>, <u>Parsifal</u>
(26) <u>Art and Revolution</u>, <u>Opera and Drama</u>,
     <u>The Art-Work of the Future</u>
(27) Gesamtkunstwerk
(28) Leitmotiv
(29) <u>The Ring of the Nibelung</u>, <u>Das Rheingold</u>,
     <u>Die Walkuere</u>, <u>Siegfried</u>, <u>Goetterdaem-
     merung</u>
(30) <u>Tristan and Isolde</u>
(31) <u>Die Meistersinger</u>
(32) Immense
(33) Verdi, Berlioz
(34) Brahms
(35) <u>Elijah</u>, <u>St. Paul</u>,
     <u>L'Enfance du Christ</u>
          ****
          (1) M   (6) M
          (2) C   (7) G
          (3) M   (8) G
          (4) C   (9) C
          (5) L   (10) M

(1) Verdi	(6) Bellini	(11) Bizet
(2) Puccini	(7) Verdi	(12) Rossini
(3) Wagner	(8) Verdi	(13) St.-Saens
(4) Rossini	(9) Weber	(14) Verdi
(5) Beethoven	(10) Wagner	(15) Wagner

LISTENING

EXAMPLE 1:	EXAMPLE 2:	EXAMPLE 3:
(1) A	(1) B	(1) A
(2) B	(2) A	(2) A
(3) A	(3) A	(3) B
(4) A	(4) A	(4) A
(5) B	(5) B	(5) A

CHAPTER TWENTY-THREE

(1) Nationalistic
(2) France, Italy, Germany, Austria
(3) Folk Songs
(4) Dance
(5) Opera, Instrumental
(6) Guitar
(7) Russia, Glinka, <u>A</u> <u>Life</u> <u>for</u>
   <u>the</u> <u>Tsar</u>, <u>Russlan</u> <u>and</u> <u>Ludmilla</u>
(8) Balakirev, Cui, Borodin,
   Mussorgsky, Rimsky-Korsakov
(9) Mussorgsky, <u>Boris</u> <u>Goudonov</u>
(10) Piano, Ravel
(11) Bohemia
(12) Smetana, <u>The</u> <u>Bartered</u> <u>Bride</u>
(13) Dvorak, Slavonic,
   <u>From</u> <u>the</u> <u>New</u> <u>World</u>
(14) Albeniz, <u>Iberia</u>
(15) Falla, Piano, <u>The</u> <u>Three-Cornered</u> <u>Hat</u>
(16) Elgar, <u>Pomp</u> <u>and</u> <u>Circumstance</u>
(17) Vaughan Williams
(18) Holst
(19) Grieg, <u>Peer</u> <u>Gynt</u>
(20) Sibelius, <u>Finlandia</u>
(21) Wagner, Mahler, Bruckner,
   Richard Strauss
(22) Symphonies, Thousand
(23) <u>Lieder</u> <u>eines</u> <u>fahrenden</u> <u>Gesellen</u>
(24) Symphonic, <u>Salome</u>
(25) Faure, Rachmaninov
         ****
(1) Spain   (6) Czechoslovakia
(2) England   (7) Russia
(3) Norway   (8) England
(4) Russia   (9) Spain
(5) Finland   (10) Czechoslovakia
         ****

LISTENING

EXAMPLE 1:   EXAMPLE 2:
(1) B   (1) B
(2) B   (2) A
(3) B   (3) A
(4) B   (4) B
(5) A   (5) A

 (1) Cubism, Picasso
 (2) Miro, Dali, Ernst
 (3) Joyce, _Ulysses_
 (4) Diaghilev, Graham
 (5) Impressionism, Debussy
 (6) Objectively
 (7) Primitive
 (8) Futurism
 (9) Gebrauchsmusik
(10) Jazz
(11) Neo-Classicism
(12) Atonality
(13) Serialism
(14) Expressionism
(15) Musique Concrete, Electronic
(16) Length, Range, Tonal
(17) Whole-tone, Pentatonic, Modes
(18) Ostinato
(19) Meter
(20) Bitonality, Polytonality
(21) Pointillism
(22) Bimodality
(23) Percussive
(24) France
(25) Griffes
(26) Boulanger
(27) Gershwin, _Rhapsody in Blue_
(28) Barber, Piston
(29) Sessions
(30) Ives, Cowell

****

(1) R		(6) T	
(2) T		(7) R	
(3) R		(8) T	
(4) T		(9) R	
(5) T		(10) T	

 (1) Painting
 (2) Symbolist
 (3) Debussy
 (4) Nature
 (5) Chord Stream
 (6) 9ths, 11ths, 13ths
 (7) Whole-tone
 (8) Flute, Clarinet, Violin,
     Horn, Trumpet
 (9) <u>Prelude</u> <u>a</u> <u>'L'Apres-midi</u> <u>d'un</u> <u>faun</u>
(10) <u>La</u> <u>Mer</u>, <u>Pelleas</u> <u>et</u> <u>Melisande</u>
(11) Preludes, <u>Feux</u> <u>d'artifice</u>
(12) "Les Six", Honegger, Milhaud, Poulenc
(13) Satie
(14) Ravel
(15) Bolero

****

 (1) Ravel   (6) Milhaud
 (2) Debussy   (7) Poulenc
 (3) Milhaud   (8) Honegger
 (4) Debussy   (9) Debussy
 (5) Honegger   (10) Debussy

****

LISTENING

EXAMPLE 1:   EXAMPLE 2:
(1) B   (1) A
(2) B   (2) B
(3) B   (3) B
(4) B   (4) A
(5) B   (5) B

CHAPTER TWENTY-SIX

 (1) Bartok, Hindemith, Stravinsky
 (2) Ives, Copland
 (3) Folk, Peasant
 (4) Liszt, Richard Strauss, Stravinsky
 (5) Simple, Pentatonic, Whole-Tone,
     Folk
 (6) Octave Displacement
 (7) Polyrhythms
 (8) Tone Cluster
 (9) Motivic
(10) Pianist, Teacher
(11) Rimsky-Korsakov
(12) Ballet
(13) Variation
(14) Ostinato, Meter, Polyrhythm
(15) Dynamic, Tempo
(16) Neoclassicism, <u>Pulcinella</u>,
     <u>Oedipus Rex</u>
(17) Gebrauchsmusik
(18) Musical Composition
(19) Quartal
(20) Conservative
(21) Tonality
(22) Insurance
(23) Unplayable
(24) Hymns, Songs, Songs, Classics
(25) Sterophonic
(26) 4, 150
(27) Boulanger
(28) Jazzlike, Dissonances, Jewish
(29) Motives, Materials
(30) Rhythmic
(31) Tonal
(32) Dance
(33) Britten
(34) Formalism
(35) Prokofiev, Shostakovich
             ****

 (1) Prokofiev   (6) Copland
 (2) Bartok   (7) Ives
 (3) Hindemith   (8) Stravinsky
 (4) Stravinsky   (9) Ives
 (5) Britten   (10) Copland

LISTENING

EXAMPLE 1:
   (1) B
   (2) A
   (3) B
   (4) B
   (5) A

EXAMPLE 2:
   (1) B
   (2) B
   (3) B
   (4) B
   (5) A

EXAMPLE 3:
   (1) B
   (2) A
   (3) B
   (4) A
   (5) B

EXAMPLE 4:
   (1) B
   (2) B
   (3) A
   (4) B
   (5) B

EXAMPLE 5:
   (1) A
   (2) A
   (3) A
   (4) A
   (5) B

CHAPTER TWENTY-SEVEN

 (1) Atonality
 (2) Schoenberg
 (3) Brahms, Wagner
 (4) Tonal
 (5) Expressionist
 (6) Sprechstimme
 (7) Klangfarbenmelodie
 (8) Serialism, Dodecaphony,
     Chromatic
 (9) Tone Row, Original, Retrograde,
     Inversion, Retrograde Inversion
(10) Teacher
(11) Berg, Lyricism
(12) Hauptstimme, Nebenstimme
(13) Webern, Classical
(14) Short
(15) Pointillism

****
 (1) S
 (2) B
 (3) B
 (4) W
 (5) S
****

LISTENING

EXAMPLE 1:	EXAMPLE 2:	EXAMPLE 3:
(1) B	(1) B	(1) A
(2) B	(2) A	(2) A
(3) B	(3) B	(3) B
(4) B	(4) B	(4) B
(5) B	(5) B	(5) A

CHAPTER TWENTY-EIGHT

 (1) Schoenberg, Bartok, Hindemith,
     Stravinsky
 (2) Paris, Messiaen
 (3) Hindu, Oriental, Palindromes
 (4) Total Serialization
 (5) Boulez, Rhythmic
 (6) Stockhausen
 (7) Cantata, 1952
 (8) Babbitt
 (9) Musique Concrete, Tape Music
(10) Varese
(11) Oscillators, Synthesizers
(12) Columbia-Princeton
(13) Computer
(14) Davidowskyd
(15) Varese
(16) Cage, Prepared
(17) Penderecki
(18) Les Noces, L'Histoire du Soldat
(19) Berio, Circles
(20) Crumb, Madrigals, Ancient
     Voices of Children
(21) Microtonality, Partch
(22) Chance, Indeterminacy, Aleatoric
(23) Changes
(24) Time
(25) Carter
(26) Minimalism
(27) Asian, Cage
(28) Riley, Glass
(29) Internationalism
(30) Hillis, Caldwell, Musgrave

****

(1)	Crumb	(6)	Stravinsky
(2)	Cage	(7)	Boulez
(3)	Babbitt	(8)	Ussachevsky
(4)	Davidkowsky	(9)	Stockhausen
(5)	Penderecki	(10)	Brown

****

LISTENING

EXAMPLE 1:	EXAMPLE 2:	EXAMPLE 3:	EXAMPLE 4:
(1) B	(1) B	(1) A	(1) A
(2) B	(2) B	(2) B	(2) B
(3) B	(3) A	(3) B	(3) B
(4) B	(4) B	(4) A	(4) B
(5) C	(5) B	(5) B	(5) B

 (1) Folk, Soul, Jazz, Country, Rock
 (2) Anglo-American, Black
 (3) England, Scotland
 (4) Orally
 (5) Words
 (6) Ballad, Stanzas, Refrain
 (7) Guitar, Banjo, Dulcimer
 (8) Dancing, Marching
 (9) Germany, France, Poland, Russia
(10) Field Holler, Group Work
(11) Ring Shout
(12) Lining Out
(13) Blues
(14) Spiritual
(15) Gospel Hymns
(16) Minstrel, Vaudeville
(17) Jazz
(18) Syncopation, Improvisation
(19) Ragtime, Scott Joplin
(20) New Orleans, Storyville
(21) Bolden, Morton, Oliver, Armstrong
(22) Beiderbecke
(23) Combos
(24) Big Band, Swing, Henderson,
     Ellington
(25) Arrangements
(26) Bop, Parker, Gillespie
(27) Cool, Davis
(28) Third Stream, John Lewis,
     Gunther Schuller
(29) Operetta, Herbert, Romberg
(30) Cohan, Comedy
(31) Berlin, Kern, Rodgers, Bernstein
(32) Grand Ole Opry
(33) Western Swing, Honky-Tonk
(34) Bluegrass
(35) Rockabilly
(36) Elvis Presley
(37) Beatles
(38) Rolling Stones
(39) Operas
(40) Punk, New Wave, Heavy Metal
          ****

 (1) Country-Western   (6) Blues
 (2) Bop   (7) Jazz
 (3) Musical Comedy   (8) Third Stream
 (4) Folk-Protest   (9) Swing
 (5) Ragtime   (10) Rock & Roll

LISTENING

EXAMPLE 1:
  (1) B
  (2) B
  (3) A
  (4) C
  (5) A

EXAMPLE 2:
  (1) B
  (2) A
  (3) A
  (4) A
  (5) B

EXAMPLE 3:
  (1) B
  (2) B
  (3) A
  (4) B
  (5) A

175

 (1) Religious, Dances, Ceremonies,
     Entertainment
 (2) Unifying
 (3) Central, Sub-Saharan
 (4) Tonal, Pitches
 (5) Responsorial
 (6) Parallel, Imitation, Drone
 (7) Polyphony
 (8) Range, Complex, Pulsating
 (9) Dances
(10) Meaningless
(11) Incomplete
(12) Plains, Six, Seven
(13) Recitative
(14) Ragas, Talas
(15) Note, Chord
(16) Physical, Intellectual
(17) Sitar, Tambura
(18) Tabla
(19) Ya-Yueh, Su-Yueh
(20) Pentatonic

****

LISTENING

EXAMPLE 1:	EXAMPLE 2:	EXAMPLE 3:
(1) A	(1) B	(1) A
(2) A	(2) B	(2) B
(3) B	(3) B	(3) B
(4) B	(4) A	(4) B
(5) A	(5) A	(5) B